Was it a cruel joke—or something more sinister?

"After each one of these little practical jokes, we have received a strange little message. I'd like your opinion." Gerald seemed to be speaking reluctantly, making a decision. He reached inside the breast pocket of his jacket and produced a small sheaf of papers. "Here. Read these."

Dewey leafed quickly through the small pile. There wasn't much to read—they were brief messages. "Monica was here," read one. "Love from Monica," read another. There were eight or ten of them, all in the same vein. At the bottom of each one was a drawing of a skull and crossbones.

Dewey gave Sonia a stern look. "You should report these to the police."

Sonia looked pained. "That's just it, Dewey. We can't bear to do that . . . If word of this got out, it would ruin us. No. You have to help us. You have to use that famous detective ability of yours, and get to the bottom of it. And save us . . ."

WANTED: DUDE OR ALIVE

KATE MORGAN

BERKLEY PRIME CRIME, NEW YORK

For Charlie and his girl

This book is a Berkley Prime Crime original edition,
and has never been previously published.

WANTED: DUDE OR ALIVE

A Berkley Prime Crime Book / published by arrangement with
the author

PRINTING HISTORY
Berkley Prime Crime edition / August 1994

ISBN: 0-425-14330-9

Berkley Prime Crime Books are published by
The Berkley Publishing Group,
200 Madison Avenue, New York, NY 10016.
The name BERKLEY PRIME CRIME and the BERKLEY PRIME CRIME
design are trademarks belonging to Berkley Publishing Corporation.

PRINTED IN THE UNITED STATES OF AMERICA

10 9 8 7 6 5 4 3 2 1

1

THE FABLED HACIENDA LOS LOBOS is tucked away among the green and brown hillsides of the Escondida Valley, close to the border with Mexico and not far from the sleepy little town of Edmunds. The Hacienda has been there longer than the town, longer than any other place within three hundred miles. It has about it an air of grave antiquity as well as opulence; it is the product of a calmer, slower, more deliberate era, when people were born at home and died at home, when people lived on what they could produce through hard work and ingenuity.

For over two centuries Los Lobos was more than just a private house. It was the domain of the rich, powerful, industrious, and unscrupulous Torcaza family. In effect— with its dozens of ranch hands and farmhands, its orchards and vineyards, its livestock and its household staff—Los Lobos was more like a small corporation than a family home.

Those days are gone, of course. Today Los Lobos survives thanks to its transformation into a deluxe inn, where people come to sample another way of life. Some customers like it so much that they come back again and again.

Here, during the month of April, eight people were gathered on the flagstone terrace under an enormous and ancient magnolia. Looking at these vacationers, in their splendid surroundings, it would be easy to forget that Los Lobos was once a place of industry rather than relaxation;

but the dead-and-gone Torcazas would have been astonished to see so many people lounging around, not doing any work at all. We live in an era of repose—no matter what we tell ourselves.

On that April morning, Dewey James, sexagenarian semiretired librarian, was one of the loungers. Feeling slightly ridiculous in an oversized straw hat, she sipped her café con leche and looked at her fellow guests with a degree of interest that bordered on nosiness. It was the end of the high season at the Hacienda, and the sojourners were fewer and slightly less glamorous than usual—during the peak of the travel season, the place was jammed with jet-setters, but the group here today seemed to Dewey to be rather down-to-earth. She wondered how easily they spooked.

The youngish woman with dark glasses was a lawyer—family law, which Dewey guessed meant divorce. The woman's husband was tall and thin, with an anxious air; he sipped suspiciously at a cup of tepid herbal tea. To Dewey's way of thinking, he didn't look or act much like a stockbroker, although that was what he claimed to be. Dewey had heard him say that he was the head of a citizens' committee to restrict the use of bicycles in California to Saturdays and Sundays. Milton was their name. They weren't having much fun, and it seemed likely that they were congenital sourpusses. Dewey studied Belinda Milton's heavy jaw and began to feel a little sorry for opposing counsel.

The other couple were familiar to Dewey, as they were to probably two or three million others. They were Serena and Lorenzo Lee, famous around the country as the buoyant hosts of "In the Field," an educational nature program that had enjoyed mild success on the public TV stations. Both were avid wildlife photographers, and they brimmed with good-natured enthusiasm—chiefly, as far as Dewey could tell, on behalf of the insect and arachnid populations of the valley.

They kept with them at all moments an enormous amount of camera equipment, including a huge, fat lens the size of a small cannon. For getting the niceties of termite society in focus, Dewey supposed. In addition to having a successful TV show, they had published their photographs everywhere, from *Ranger Rick* to *National Geographic*. They were chatting merrily with Dewey's good friend and present traveling companion, George Farnham. He appeared to be getting a kick out of them.

In real life, Serena was quite plain, her plainness exaggerated by her deliberately drab clothing. Very likely she felt the need to wear camouflage, Dewey reflected, so as not to frighten the fauna. Serena went everywhere in a pair of falling-apart Birkenstock sandals, and she had an overbearing air of good sense that could be described as bordering on the bossy—and which occasionally crossed that line. To Dewey, Serena seemed vaguely Central European, an impression that was heightened by her very precise, almost uninflected English, with no trace of an accent. Dewey's mind conjured up an image of the tense moment at the ball in *My Fair Lady:* "I can tell that she was born—Hungarian!" Well, Serena was possibly Hungarian, Dewey reflected, but probably not of royal blood. Not in those shoes.

Dewey had heard Lorenzo's voice a hundred times, but she realized now that for his show he used a stage voice. Here on the terrace at Los Lobos, his accent was pure Brooklyn. His sparkling gray-blue eyes had a mischievous look, and he struck Dewey as being almost impish. His remarks thus far—at the dinner table last night, where all the guests had met for the first time, and at breakfast this morning—had hinted at a strong streak of fantasy, kept carefully under wraps lest it irritate the good, solid common sense of his wife. Dewey reckoned that Lorenzo might be a bit of an amateur philosopher from time to time; she imagined his philosophy might be creative rather than rigorous.

They were a devoted couple, or so it appeared, always stopping in their conversations to seek out each other's opinions on the smallest matter. It seemed to Dewey that life with Serena and Lorenzo would be a slow process, with constant breaks in the action to take a vote, to find reassurance, to get the necessary go-ahead.

On the opposite side of the terrace, next to a thriving purple bougainvillea, was Mark Harris, the tennis pro at Los Lobos. About thirty, medium-tall, with medium brown hair, Harris was rather anonymous; when you looked at him, you tended to see the tennis whites rather than the man. As far as Dewey could tell, he kept more or less to himself, only arriving to mingle when he was about to give a lesson or have a game. Dewey wasn't much of a tennis player herself, but George Farnham loved the game. Perhaps he could play this week.

Seated next to Harris was a tall, glamorous-looking woman of about sixty. Her hair was golden, with a few unobtrusive streaks of gray; her extremely tasteful clothes, for all their outdoorsiness, were obviously expensive; and her air was that of someone who had seen it all and could have whatever she wanted. Dewey had recognized her in an instant. This was Eloise Morningside, the editor of *Faces* magazine.

In thirty years of publication, *Faces* had turned basest gossip into a more-or-less respectable commodity; and Eloise had been on board since the beginning. She had taken the helm of the magazine at the tender age of thirty, and it was fair to estimate that, by now, she knew absolutely everyone—and, more importantly, she knew everything about them. Eloise seemed to have an instinct for finding out the personal details in the lives of famous people; these secrets she exposed skillfully, whetting the public's appetite for more.

Eloise (the whole world knew her by her first name) could have been a first-class jet-setter had she chosen, but in her shrewdness she had elected to be famous for her reticence. She kept herself out of the news, and she kept her personal history quiet—her style demanded it. It was typical of Eloise to take a low-profile, publicity-free vacation, somehow becoming all the more glamorous by playing it down. Today she was dressed in a simple little tennis outfit that Dewey knew must have cost a fortune; she was swinging her racquet, ready for her morning lesson from Harris. Dewey had learned last night, over coffee in the red-velvet parlor, that Eloise Morningside was quite a player.

It might have seemed surprising to some people that Dewey James was here with these high-fliers—for she was a quiet-living librarian, and semiretired to boot. But Dewey was here gratis, by special invitation. A week at Los Lobos was, of course, far beyond the reach of her modest budget. In her comfortable, creaky frame house in Hamilton, two thousand miles to the north and east in the luscious green countryside of the Boone River Valley, she thought of herself as being tolerably well-off. But here among the rich and famous she was keenly aware of the limitations of her means—a small widow's pension (her husband had been Hamilton's chief of police) and an equally small salary, which she earned through her diligence at the Hamilton Public Library. Dewey had not the smallest objection to going first-class for free.

She was earning her keep. One might not know it to look at her—her sparkling blue eyes, her well-worn, casual attire, and her general air of insouciance—but Dewey James was a woman with a mission. She had come to the

Escondida Valley on assignment, as it were. Remembering her job, she sat up straighter in her chair and did her best not to look like a spy.

In the Hacienda's famous kitchen, a heated discussion was taking place. It was here, around a large, rough-looking refectory table, that the Los Lobos professional staff gathered most mornings to eat breakfast and to talk over the projects for the coming day or week. Depending on the guests, the activities at Los Lobos varied, of course, but generally speaking it was Charles Halifax, head of the stables, who outlined the projects for the day.

Charles was rude to almost everyone, except the guests; with them, he was merely insolent and occasionally lightly offensive. Despite these personal failings, Gerald kept him on; there was no question that Halifax knew horses, and he managed a large part of the Hacienda's breeding operation, which was a lucrative and important sideline for Gerald and Sonia Clearwater.

Charles this morning was being rude to Harriet Bray, a tiresomely vivacious woman in her late twenties who had originally been hired as his assistant. Recently, she had also taken over the Hacienda's athletic programs, such as they were. Unfortunately, most of the people who came to Los Lobos had no time for aerobics or weight machines. Such things were part of the workaday world; the guests at Los Lobos came to the Escondida Valley precisely to escape the conscientious efforts of their personal trainers. They tended to ride in the mornings, play a little tennis in the late afternoon, and drink a lot of gin on the terrace at sunset. Nobody wanted any part of Harriet's aerobics classes. Occasionally, Charles allowed her to ride—this was what she longed to do, and why she had taken the job. But generally it pleased him to ignore her altogether.

Today Harriet was dressed in a vibrantly colored aerobics outfit—top, tights, warm-up jacket, pert little socks, and the latest in footgear. Everything she wore was perfectly coordinated; she had about fifteen such outfits, all designed to show off her sleek, fit body. Her skin had a healthy flush, because she had just completed her vigorous personal workout. Her good health spread outward—like radiation from a mushroom cloud, thought Charles Halifax. He wished he could live in a bomb shelter, away from the determined sunniness of her. He wished he were a smoker, a heavy, heavy smoker, just so he could light up and keep her at bay.

"I hate to tell you, Charles, but I'm supposed to be more than your personal slave," Harriet complained. "And nobody ever wants to take aerobics. For once, I'd like a chance to take some people out riding. In case you forgot, I'm a riding instructor. I'm only doing the aerobics to fill in for Monica." She took a bite of her small health muffin and glared disapprovingly at his plate.

Charles, to annoy Harriet, had taken to ordering enormous breakfasts—three eggs, six slices of bacon, English muffins dripping with butter and honey, fresh fruit, juice, and strong coffee with cream and sugar. She was allergic to about half the things on his plate—Harriet was famous for her allergies, and extremely particular about her food. Her allergies were one of the dull conversational veins that she liked to mine. The others were similar—the lipid contents of certain foods and the dangers of gluten were two of her other favorites. Charles detested her talk.

He reached for another piece of bacon with his stubby fingers, giving an involuntary glance toward his expanding belly. At forty-five, he found it difficult to keep trim, in spite of the many hours of exercise he got each day. His jodhpurs were beginning to feel seriously tight, a bad sign. But he was loath to give up the pleasure of tormenting Harriet. He'd just have to sneak into the sauna while she was out on one of her earnest nature walks, or counting sit-ups in the gym.

"Charles. I want to take these people out." Harriet's voice was a whine.

He stuffed the greasy bacon into his mouth and looked at her. "Don't be ridiculous," he said, his mouth still full. "Have you taken a look at them? They're not exactly the Lone Ranger type."

Harriet knew Charles was right, but she didn't rise to the bait. She glowered, and he went offensively on.

"I mean you can take your pick. Mr. and Mrs. Tarantula from Transylvania—they don't ride, they probably spin webs in their spare time. Or Mr. and Mrs. Doom-and-gloom, who'd probably depress the hell out of the horses. I don't think we can risk it. The old biddy from East Podunk and her boyfriend—I doubt they know the front end of a horse from the back. And then of course there's the fabulous Eloise. You won't get far with her. She's fabulous, and she doesn't ride, and if she did, she certainly wouldn't be caught dead riding with you. She's far too fabulous, and she doesn't have time for people like you, Harriet."

Harriet admitted, but only to herself, that there weren't many prospects in the group. Well, if she couldn't take anybody riding, maybe she could tempt them to take an aerobics class. Or even go on a nature hike with her. Maybe the nature photographers would like her to take them hiking—but probably not. They could go on their own and probably do better. They were experts, and she was just someone who liked to wander around outside, looking at things and trying to understand them.

Halifax snickered. "So why don't you just relax? Enjoy the fact that you get a full salary for doing half a job." He stabbed at a fried egg, and the yolk began to run. "And for God's sake don't try anything behind my back. If and when I want you to take people out on my horses, I'll let you know. Now stop pestering me about it."

Halifax, although he was thoroughly obnoxious, had a point—Harriet's enthusiasm was aggressive, and other people felt it. Harriet was working too hard to be one of the gang, when she was really in over her head. It would have been smart to sit back and let Charles invite her to do things. Instead, she asked to be part of the fun, and Charles, to be perverse, snubbed her. That was his way.

Harriet Bray was fighting a losing battle. With her attitude, she belonged at a health spa, not at Los Lobos, a place more famous for indulgence than for abstinence. But she didn't need Charles to remind her. He was nothing but a disgusting, complacent slob. Well, if he was going to be obnoxious, she could be obnoxious, too.

"I thought we were selling Cerveza. Mark told me that he thinks the sale fell through."

Halifax frowned. "Mark Harris should mind his own business. He doesn't know anything about the stables. That's my job. Tell him to mind his own business."

"The success of Los Lobos is everybody's business," replied Harriet, in an irritating singsong. "That makes three sales that haven't gone through. I hope Gerald isn't too mad about it."

"Gerald doesn't know anything about it," replied Halifax. "Neither does Mark Harris. Neither do you, Harriet." He smiled blandly at her.

She glowered in return. "You're getting fat, Charles. Soon you'll be too fat to ride, and some poor horse will break in two, and you'll fall down the mountainside and break your thick neck. All because you stuff your face to spite me, because you think I'm your social inferior."

Halifax smiled. "I don't just think so. You *are*, my dear. Sorry—there's nothing to be done about it. You simply must accept the little injustices of life."

2

On Santa Maria Avenue, right in the heart of Edmunds, not much was happening. It was a hot day, and that was putting it mildly. On one corner, in the shade of a two-story building, a one-eyed, black-and-white dog was lounging, chin on paws, watching the pickups and the station wagons full of grimy kids pull into the Dairy Squeeze parking lot. Across the street at Terry's Towing and Garage, Terry was sitting in front of a brand-new electric fan, steadily ignoring a customer waiting for gasoline. The True Value Hardware affiliate boasted coolers and barbecues to beat the heat. Down the street at Mike's Donut-O-Rama, enormous flies buzzed languidly around a sticky pot of strawberry jelly.

Right in the center of all this hustle and bustle were the offices of the *Foothill Trumpeter*, the only newspaper serving the towns of Edmunds and Villaseca. The office, with its large glass window taking the full force of the afternoon sunshine, was small, cramped, and hot. Even on the coolest days, little fresh air penetrated into the cheaply paneled room on Santa Maria. An overhead fan hung still and silent above the small room.

The occupant of this noxious room was Larry Ceboll, publisher and editor of the *Trumpeter*. He didn't mind the stale air, the reek of the smoke of countless cheap cigars, the worn patches in the rust-colored indoor/outdoor carpet, or the places where the wood paneling on the walls bulged and threatened to pry loose from its nails. Larry Ceboll kind of liked things this way—it kept people away. He didn't like people to come around, volunteering their time and their oh-so-interesting articles on dahlias or dog care or the local economy or the problem of reliable, legal domestic help. Larry Ceboll liked to run the *Trumpeter* more or less as an extension of his personality—and, generally speaking, his approach worked. Like Larry Ceboll, the *Foothill Trumpeter* was disagreeable, offensive, and difficult to ignore.

He adjusted the sweat-stained khaki shirt that strained across his middle, lit a cheap cigar, grunted, and glanced at his watch. The sheriff would come by at four-thirty, bringing his weekly list of police activity for the crime column. It would be the usual: a couple of anonymous farm workers doing an overnight in jail for D & D, maybe an accident or two, and a stolen vehicle. The regular weekly stuff, plus maybe something in the way of real news. Last week there had been some kind of vandalism, down at the only non-Catholic church in town. That had filled two columns, what with needing to write about religious intolerance and figuring out how to irritate equally the people on both sides. Larry Ceboll liked to be fair.

Despite his evenhanded policies, Ceboll didn't have many friends in this town of 11,000. He never had, not as a boy, and not as a man. His own father had given up trying to like him long ago; his mother had died giving birth to a second child, a girl, who had been adopted by a family back East. That was just as well, really, because little Larry had been a monster. He would have blighted the life of any sibling, so disagreeable was he as a child.

As a man, he was more disagreeable than ever. Larry Ceboll didn't give a damn whether or not he had friends. If you were powerful enough, you didn't really need them. He was a big landowner—not huge, not like some of the ranchers and farmers, who still had significant holdings in the area. But still he was big enough, because he owned nearly all of what passed for commercial real estate here in Edmunds, plus most of downtown Villaseca, the next town over. He charged exorbitant rents to Terry's garage, to Mike's Donut-O-Rama, and to the True Value affiliate. He charged a fortune—comparatively speaking—for the little office where one of the town's three lawyers practiced. Ceboll chuckled. That was one lawyer who'd never get rich. Well, it was immigration law, mostly, of course, and half those people couldn't pay. The lawyer stayed, though, just like Terry and Mike and the guy in the hardware place.

Larry Ceboll leaned back in his chair and wondered, for about the ninetieth time in three weeks, if maybe he shouldn't consider kicking the lawyer out. The lawyer's name—Shinefeld, or something like that—was a dead giveaway. Not that Ceboll especially minded Jews. No, it was nothing like that at all. Ceboll hated everybody pretty equally, whether they were Jews, Catholics, Protestants, Navajo, Mexicans, non-Mexicans, whoever.

It was just that Ceboll figured that Jews were generally Democrats, and Democrat lawyers usually had connections with the ACLU and/or whoever, all those pussyfooting, trouble-making groups that Larry Ceboll could live without. Before you knew it, Ceboll thought, that little squirt would be holding town meetings, or running for municipal office, or getting people hyped about unfair monopolies in commercial real estate. Ceboll puffed on his cigar and thought some more about how to kick the annoying little Democrat squirt of a lawyer out of his office. It was an enjoyable problem.

A bell tinkled as the glass-paned door pushed open.

"Afternoon, Mr. Ceboll," said Sheriff Packy Tate, waving away the flies that circled near the door and making his way into the cramped little office. Like Ceboll, Tate was fiftyish, fat, and grayish, but the resemblance ended there. Tate was neither a landowner nor a media mogul; unlike Ceboll, he was viewed with yawning indifference by most of the citizens of Edmunds. He was faithfully reelected every five years precisely because the populace had no feeling about him, one way or another; in a town and county that were basically free of crime, there wasn't much call for a big-shot sheriff. Plus, there was nobody else who much wanted the ten-thousand-dollar-a-year job. Too much like work. But Packy Tate, with his limited vision and his even more limited intelligence, was perfect for the position.

In spite of it all, however, Packy Tate was a pretty good sheriff. He tried to be conscientious, and he did his best not to play favorites between the two types of people in town who generally came his way—the farm workers and the redneck kids. There were plenty of illegal aliens living shadowy lives in and around Edmunds and Villaseca, but Packy Tate had always figured that the illegals weren't his problem, so long as they didn't commit crimes. He wasn't about to try to kick them out; that kind of headache he left to the INS. Mr. Ceboll wanted to keep the INS out of Edmunds, so Packy Tate never worried about the illegals. He liked to oblige his constituents. His forbearance won him the appreciation of both the workers and the major land-owners in the vicinity; this appreciation was about the only sentiment he ever excited in the hearts and minds of the people of Edmunds.

"Hi, Tate," said Ceboll, sliding his cigar into a corner of his mouth and talking around it. "Got anything?"

"Naw, just the regular, Mr. Ceboll." Tate approached the desk. "Coupla vehicles, coupla D & Ds, one guy reported a backhoe stolen, then he found it." Tate slapped a single sheet of paper down on the desk in front of Ceboll. It was a shiny photocopy of the handwritten police log for the week.

Ceboll picked the paper up and glanced over it quickly. Tate shifted back and forth from one foot to the other. Ceboll gave him a look of curiosity. "You got something else."

"Nothing, really." He looked at his feet.

Ceboll looked hard at Tate. The publisher of the *Foothill Trumpeter* owned a large promissory note signed by Tate. Ceboll didn't need the money, didn't care about the money, and so Packy Tate hadn't made more than just a few payments on the note. But the note came in handy whenever Ceboll needed the law and order in town to go his way. Ceboll would have liked it if Packy Tate never made another payment at all. Then the law in this town would really be sewn up.

"You got something else," Ceboll repeated.

Tate took off his hat and twirled it around in his hands. "Just a rumor, Mr. Ceboll. Nothing for the paper."

"I'll decide what's a rumor and what's a fact around here."

Tate swallowed hard. "Something I heard about things up at Los Lobos yesterday morning."

"Ahh." Ceboll took the cigar out of his mouth and leaned forward. It was no secret that Ceboll wanted Los Lobos in the worst way. He lusted after it. That property had everything: good fields, vineyards, an orchard of apricot trees, a great view, and—best of all—water. Two springs, a stream, and a small lake. Would be worth a fortune to the right buyer. Tear down that old house, and that idiot chapel, and put up some luxury condos. He knew a good contractor who would build there real cheap. It would be a piece of cake. Ceboll pressed forward in his chair. "What?"

"I don't think I should tell you."

"Tate, Tate, Tate. You're so stupid about these things." Ceboll opened his desk drawer, the one where he kept Tate's promissory note. He always kept it handy, so that he could use it like a lever or a crowbar whenever it suited him. He smiled, showing yellow teeth, and waved the note.

"Listen, Mr. Ceboll, you been pullin' that note outta there for the last eight years. You gotta stop with that. I think I'll just pay it off."

"Huh-uh-unh," taunted Ceboll, waving the note. "Worth more to me now than ever." He turned the paper around and looked at it. "Besides, Packy, where the hell would you get eight thousand dollars?"

"Been savin'," Tate responded lamely. It was true that he would never be able to get his hands on the eight thousand. Not all at once. And Packy Tate wasn't the kind of guy who could put his dollars aside one at a time and watch them mount up. A born spender, he was.

"If you've got something that might help me get my hands on that place, Packy, I swear to you I'll tear this thing up."

"Uh, Mr. Ceboll—"

"I know you don't believe me. I know you've done other favors for me, and maybe you shouldn't have. 'Cause now, look. You don't believe me."

"Well, not really," Tate admitted. He wasn't very good at pretending.

"Well, you should believe me. Scout's honor." Ceboll held up his right hand in a parody of the Scout salute, then burst into a long, heavy laugh, which ended unattractively in a wheeze and a cough.

Maybe Ceboll would die, thought Packy Tate, and then he could sneak in here one day, open that drawer up, and burn that darned note.

When Ceboll had finished wheezing and coughing, he

glared at Tate. "So help me, Packy, you'd better tell me what's goin' on. Maybe I can help."

Packy Tate looked at his feet. "It's that girl," he said.

"Which one? The one in the pink jumpsuits all the time?"

"Her? Naw, I heard she's the new gym teacher up there. Nope, I mean the other one, the old gym teacher, the one that drownded up there."

"Probably done in by some—"

"That's the one," Tate interrupted. He hated Ceboll's language. "And everybody's still talking about it, a whole month later, even though the medical examiner said it was an accident."

Ceboll grunted and his eyes lit up. He had never believed that story. Girls didn't just turn up dead from accidents. Besides, wasn't she supposed to be an athlete? He had always thought there would be more to the story one day. She had been pretty, that girl, and with the kind of look in her eye that usually meant trouble. Like she had ideas, big ideas, about something. She was the kind of girl Larry Ceboll had been able to relate to.

"So, Packy, did you trick somebody into giving you a confession?"

"Nope." Tate shook his head resignedly, oblivious to the irony behind Ceboll's question. "But I got this in my office, just the other day." From his shirt pocket he produced a folded-up envelope. He unfolded it and withdrew a brief letter, typewritten on a crumpled, dirty piece of paper. "I don't know, Mr. Ceboll. It ain't news. But maybe you can tell me what you think about this." He handed it over to Ceboll.

Dear Sheriff Tate,

I think you should check up on that girl Monica that died up at Los Lobos. You been fooled. You should make those people up there tell you the truth. Ask them about her ghost. Ask them about what's going on. That girl wants justice.

Sincerely,
A Friend

Larry Ceboll read it through quickly and raised his eyebrows. "What's all this about a ghost?"

"I don't know. I talked to Mr. Clearwater, and he said it wasn't no big deal. Somebody's playing practical jokes. But I talked to the stable hands and the maids, and some of them think it's that girl's ghost, and they're scared."

Ceboll looked gratified. "Whatcha gonna do about it, Packy?"

"Well, thing is, I still got the file on her. Her parents were mighty upset."

"Maybe they shoulda known her better. She was a troublemaker."

"Maybe." Packy Tate shrugged. "Anyway, so I called up and talked to Matt Little." Matthew Little was the Lincoln County medical examiner.

"Jeez, you got off your fat butt?"

Tate ignored him. "He's not going to change his mind, he says. That girl's death was accidental."

"My—" Ceboll swore and rubbed his dirty hands together. "You know what this means, don't you, Packy?"

"I didn't really think it meant anything, Mr. Ceboll, except that some crank wrote me a letter."

"Packy, Packy. You will always just be the sheriff around here. And I'm gonna own the whole of the Escondida Valley. And you know why? Because I've got imagination."

"But, Mr. Ceboll—"

"See, what this means, buddy boy, is that just maybe we'll be able to make ol' Larry's dream come true. Hah-

hah!" He snatched the letter out of Tate's hand and stuffed it in his desk drawer.

"Wait, Mr. Ceboll, you gotta give me that back."

"No, I don't." Ceboll relit his stump of a cigar and puffed heavily on it.

"But it's evidence." Tate's protest was almost a whine.

"Evidence of what?"

"Well, it says right there I should investigate."

"Now, what you gonna investigate, Packy, if you ain't got proof that there was a crime committed?"

Packy Tate scratched his head. Somehow that question didn't seem right to him, but he couldn't quite figure out why.

"And if you don't think she was murdered, Packy—if it was an accident—how could the letter be evidence?"

"Mr. Ceboll—"

"Look," Ceboll said persuasively. "If it's evidence, I'll let you have it. Right now, it's just something for my newspaper. The public has a right to know, Packy, about the dirty little secret up at the fancy Hacienda Los Lobos."

He grinned and turned the key in the drawer, locking the letter away with Packy Tate's promissory note. He had a plan, but first he would have to get more information. That wouldn't be difficult. Larry Ceboll had a knack for getting what he wanted, and he knew who to talk to. There was no point in owning a town if you didn't know who to talk to.

3

SONIA CLEARWATER'S LETTER had arrived by overnight express and taken Dewey rather by surprise. She knew Sonia well, of course, as Sonia was George Farnham's first cousin, and they had all grown up in Hamilton together. Sonia, however, had moved to California more than forty years ago, when she married Gerald Clearwater. She had maintained her ties to Hamilton, and wrote to her friends and family fairly regularly. Every now and then, Sonia even came home to visit. So it wasn't the fact of the letter, but its urgent contents, that had surprised Dewey.

I don't know if you realize what a terrible time we went through when that young woman drowned. It was a tragic accident, and very difficult for me and Gerald particularly, because we were fond of her. But we managed to put it behind us, or so we thought.

Now—I'm sure you don't believe in ghosts any more than I do. And of course Gerald is completely dismissive. But if word gets out that there's a ghost at Los Lobos—or if this whole thing has to be dug up and gone through again—well, you know how people can be. We'll be ruined, because at this point the only thing that keeps the wolf from the door is the tourist trade. Gerald's family ran out of money at least a century ago, and my family, as you know, never had any to start with. It would be such a terrible blow to

Gerald to lose this beautiful place, after having worked
so very hard to hang on to it. He doesn't deserve that.

   We need to get to the bottom of our little problem.
We need help from someone strong-minded, sensible,
not easily frightened, who likes to ride horses, and who
can be discreet and enormously nosy at the same time.
Now—isn't that you to a T?"

Dewey wasn't sure she was "enormously nosy"—although
she did have her ways of finding out about things. Nosy
when nosiness was needed, that was all. It was true that
Dewey was particularly well suited to this type of task.
Inquisitive by nature, she also had a strong deductive
instinct, and she understood human nature rather well. She
was known locally as something of an amateur sleuth—
much to the dismay of the local Hamilton police force. She
forgave Sonia for the description and continued reading.

   Sonia went on to relate a series of sophomoric pranks that
had begun to plague the Hacienda. One guest had had his
towels and clothes stolen from his room while he was
showering; in the kitchen, the chef had been the victim of
the substitution of salt for sugar. In the stables, someone had
drenched all the horses' oats with beer—an event that could
have had terrible consequences had it not been discovered
early.

   I've interviewed the entire staff, and nobody will
confess. There's really not much I can do, short of
firing them all, because whoever it is thinks he can get
away with it. The problem is that some of the staff are
sort of superstitious, and for some crazy reason they
think we really do have a ghost. I don't particularly
care what *they* think, but they have begun to scare our
guests with these stories.

Gerald and I have decided that the only way to get rid of the ghost is to expose the prankster, but for that we need a *very* plausible double agent in our midst. Do say you'll come. Really. You're just perfect for the job. I'll be waiting for your call.

Dewey was delighted with Sonia's invitation. She looked hastily into the airline schedules and, certain she could get on a plane, called back at once to accept.

Thrilled with Sonia, the adventure, and herself, she chatted eagerly to George Farnham. But George, rather unexpectedly, had furrowed his brow.

He reached for the letter from Sonia. "May I?"

"Of course." They were in Dewey's parlor. It was a chilly evening, the last weekend in March, and the two good friends were enjoying a glass of sherry and some fine Roquefort, which George had brought over as a tribute to the promise of spring. In Dewey's garden, the rain belied the promise. Irises and tulips bent their heads under the weight of a cold rain, the kind that seems to pledge that winter will go on, unrelenting, for many months to come. Dewey was heartily sick and tired of the cold and wet; she was warmed just at the thought of the hot, sunny hillsides of the Escondida Valley. She handed him the letter from his cousin. "I am really looking forward to seeing Sonia. Look at that horrible rain coming down. Isn't it wonderful, George? A chance to get away from April showers, for once."

George Farnham remained silent, reading the letter through.

"Forgive me, Dewey," George finally said, shaking his head over the letter, "but I have to butt in here. I don't think you should go."

"Not go? To see my dear old friend Sonia, your own dear

cousin, at her exclusive and expensive ranch, for free, to help her solve a silly little problem?"

"It may sound like a silly problem in this letter," George replied, "but I'll bet you ponchos to pesos that Sonia is really worried. And, my dear, there *are* such things as ghosts."

"Oh, pooh."

Dewey fixed George with one of her stubborn looks. This was absurd—George Farnham, the most stolid citizen in all of Hamilton, claiming that he believed in ghosts. George Farnham was widely known (in Hamilton, at least) as a respectable lawyer, civic leader, and dry-eyed antisentimentalist.

"Pooh," said Dewey again.

"Don't say 'pooh,' my dear, if you know not whereof you speak."

"I do say 'pooh.' I've never seen a ghost of any kind, and neither have you."

"No," George agreed, "but plenty of people have got 'em."

"Well," said Dewey, "even if that's so—and I don't really think it *is* so—ghosts don't arrive suddenly. Sonia and Gerald have lived at Los Lobos for over forty years, and the place is more than two hundred years old. Surely if there were going to be ghosts at Los Lobos, they would have arrived centuries ago. No ghost would just turn up today."

"That depends," said George in reply, looking at his friend with serious eyes, "on whose ghost it is. Are we absolutely sure that girl's death was accidental?"

Dewey felt a chill run up her spine. She hadn't really thought about it, but it was true—there had been something unsatisfying in the investigation of the girl's death. And there had been nasty insinuations. Sonia had written a long letter to Dewey last month, relating all of the grim details.

She had been terribly distressed, because she had liked the young woman, but Monica Toro had been both beautiful and indiscriminate in her social habits. The local sheriff, who Dewey gathered was not a paragon of firmness, had kept turning up at funny times to ask peculiar questions. He had grilled Gerald Clearwater thoroughly on several occasions, and he had even wanted to close the Hacienda while he interviewed the staff. Fortunately they had been able to stop him with an injunction. The Clearwaters had felt that they were the object of some none-too-subtle persecution in the matter.

The local medical examiner had found no reason to suspect foul play; he had ruled the cause of death asphyxiation by drowning, and a local judge had ordered a safety investigation of the swimming pool in which the woman had drowned. Those measures had seemed to satisfy everyone, and eventually things had gone back to normal, without too much in the way of adverse publicity. But it had been a dreadful time for Sonia and Gerald.

Dewey brought common sense to bear on the problem. "Don't be ridiculous, George. Of course it was an accident. There was a huge and thorough investigation."

"I seem to recall that Sonia was very uneasy about the whole thing at the time. Don't you remember?"

"Of course she was uneasy. It must have been perfectly awful for her, and for everyone out there. She really liked that young woman, and it was a terrible tragedy, and now it's coming back to haunt her."

"So to speak," said George, with a stern look at his friend. "I think it sounds dangerous, Dewey. I'll call Sonia and tell her you've changed your mind."

"You'll do no such thing, you old bossy-boots." Dewey glared at George. "If you're so worried about my going out

there, then why don't you just ask Sonia if you can come
with me?"

"Hmmm."

"I knew you'd like that. This way you can protect me
from Monica's ghost, if I need to be protected, which I
won't. I'll be too busy exposing the prankster."

George had smiled, his eyes twinkling. He liked the idea
of going to Los Lobos with Dewey. The two of them would
have a whale of a time—and Los Lobos had one of the most
famous chefs in the country. The food would be marvelous,
the air warm and dry, the sunshine brilliant. Best of all,
George would make sure that his headstrong friend didn't
bite off more than she could chew—something that she was
constantly in danger of doing. George liked the idea of
saving her from herself.

"You're on, my dear. I'll call Sonia tonight. But first,
you'll come with me to the kitchen, where I'll find
something acceptable in that refrigerator of yours for our
dinner."

Now as she relaxed in the clear warm morning sunshine at
Los Lobos, Dewey thought again about that conversation
with George. The very idea of a ghost was ridiculous—
unless it was the ghost of some antique cowboy, or
conquistador, or missionary, or explorer—the ghost of
someone who had crossed these hillsides en route to the
Pacific several centuries ago. A true romantic ghost was
something Dewey could believe in, as she looked about her.
This place was just right for one of those.

The main house at Los Lobos dated from the mid-
eighteenth century, and it had been constructed over the
course of several decades. The earliest part of the structure
had once been a stable; it now served as a large and fairly
elegant dining room. The present-day butler's pantry had

been the family's rather cramped living quarters, and they had cooked in a small cook house, long gone. Gradually the Torcaza family—Gerald Clearwater's ancestors—had added to the adobe and *cal y canto* structure, until the whole was a large, C-shaped, one-story building around a cool, green central courtyard.

At the north end of the courtyard was the chapel, a red-painted stucco building with a tiny bell tower, which had been erected shortly after the completion of the house. A local priest came and heard the Mass there every Sunday, even today. According to the brochure that the Hacienda gave visitors, the chapel had been in constant use for over two hundred years. Beyond the chapel were the stables, with room for about fifty or sixty horses, although at present Gerald only had about twenty-five. In a stone outbuilding were the offices, where the business of running a luxury inn was conducted; the computer monitors and fax machines looked startlingly out of place in the cool, dark building with its mission furniture. On the other side of the main house was a modern tennis court and a small new gymnasium building.

The inn was exceedingly well run. All the furnishings were antiques, and most of them had been in Gerald's family for several generations. At night, the guests and the Clearwaters sat down together to a dinner served on Gerald's grandmother's Sèvres; they used his great-aunt's silver, and his great-grandmother's linens for the table. The bedrooms were similarly equipped with beautiful antique bed linens, chests and armoires, chairs, water pitchers, and washbasins. Three generations ago, the family had been a very large one—there had been twelve brothers and sisters, and all of them had spent their entire lives at Los Lobos, raising their children here. So there were plenty of household provisions to prettily outfit the fourteen modest guest rooms.

Dewey thought again about the young woman who had drowned. She hadn't asked Sonia about her—she had been careful, in fact, to keep a certain distance between herself and her hostess, to keep up her charade as an ordinary guest. But it seemed to Dewey that if Los Lobos was haunted, it would be haunted by the past, and not by the present, whose spirits dwelt in computers and cellular telephones.

Dewey looked across the flagged terrace toward the large wicker armchair, where George looked perfectly at home in his broad-brimmed felt hat and red-and-white checked shirt. Dewey wondered if he had really come with her out of concern for her safety. She thought perhaps his motives had been mingled—the famed Los Lobos kitchen alone had been enough to lure him to this untamed little corner of the great Southwest. But she was glad he had come. He was clearly enjoying himself, chatting genially with Serena and Lorenzo Lee on the subject of tyrant-flycatchers. George wanted to know what was tyrannical about them; the Lees were at great pains to elucidate.

George felt Dewey's gaze and winked at her, a cowboy wink. He was paying full freight for this deluxe week, and loving every minute of it. Dewey looked beyond the terrace to the old chapel. Gerald Clearwater was surveying his guests from the chapel's shaded porch. With a look, he summoned Dewey, who put down her coffee cup and slipped away to meet him on the far side of the old building.

They took seats on a wooden porch, a fairly recent addition to the house. Clearwater turned to her with pale, watery blue eyes that seemed to have trouble focusing for long on anything. His gray hair was vaguely in need of a cut, and overall he had a shaggy, surprised-looking appearance—

almost, Dewey had always thought, as though someone had mistakenly tossed him in a clothes dryer and left him to whirl about for a while.

Sonia joined them immediately, breezing in from the kitchen gardens, clippers in one hand, a huge clump of basil in the other. Sonia was still a remarkably stylish and handsome woman. Like Gerald, she was graying, but she seemed to have the process under control. Where Gerald was disheveled, she was tidy and orderly; his Hermès cravat was spotted and wrinkled, but Sonia wore a pristine Chanel scarf, beautifully tied about her long white neck.

She waved the basil at Dewey. "We're lunching Italian style," she said briskly, and drew up a chair. "Tomatoes with mozzarella and basil. People like the idea of beans and rice much more than they like the reality of beans and rice." She sat down, tossing her short-cropped hair. "So. Have you found our ghost?"

Dewey shook her head. "Not a trace." Dewey had spent the hours since her arrival obliquely observing the staff— the chef, his assistant, two grooms, a stable boy, three maids, two waiters, a handyman, and the secretary, who was also the bookkeeper. Sonia had told her that this was the skeleton crew—the bare bones of what it took to run Los Lobos. In the high season, it took twice this number to keep the guests happy. And keeping the guests happy was the name of the game at Los Lobos.

Dewey still hadn't had a chance to observe the professional staff—Mark Harris, Charles Halifax, and Harriet Bray. These people, Dewey reasoned, were likely to wonder aloud at a guest who seemed to be too curious. She would have to be more casual, more natural and less inquisitive, in her approach. Sometimes her nosy-old-lady act didn't go over so well, and Mark Harris had already caught her snooping through his tennis-lesson logbook. That had been a sticky moment, but Dewey had long ago perfected the "Who, me?" look of innocence that allowed her to get away with a great number of astonishing things.

So far, she had turned up nothing suspicious. Of course, she would learn more if she had a chance to interrogate people, in her own subtle way. But the emptiness of her observations made her wonder.

"Are you sure, Sonia, that—well, that all of these things are really connected in some way? It could all just be an unfortunate string of coincidences. I mean, maybe the chef made a mistake, and used the 'ghost' as a whipping boy, so to speak."

"And the stolen bath towels?"

"Well, let's say that the chambermaid meant to bring fresh ones and became distracted. I often leave off halfway through doing something."

Sonia smiled and shook her head. "We all do. But that's not the point, my dear. These things were deliberate."

"You can't tell me that the beer in the horses' feed was a coincidence, Dewey," Gerald put in. "Nor an accident."

"No." Sonia sounded more firm than usual. She looked intently at her old friend. "Listen, Dewey. There's no question about it. Someone is trying to ruin us."

"But surely there must be some other possible explanation."

"The problem is, Dewey, that one of these days our very particular guests are going to get wind of these crazy rumors." She sighed. "Then we'll lose our Royale Crest."

"You'll have to forgive my ignorance," said Dewey lightly, "but is that a family heirloom?"

Sonia grinned. "Hotel talk. Sorry. It's a rating, like Michelin or Cordon Bleu—we get it for being so very good at what we do." She gave her husband an amused glance.

Dewey realized that it must be difficult for Gerald to open his family home to strangers all the time, to make small talk with them, to treat them like valued friends of the family.

"It's hard work, isn't it?" she asked.

"Extremely hard," Sonia answered. "You have to be on all the time, which is really the hardest part—at least for me. Gerald is much better at it than I am. It comes more naturally to him."

Gerald Clearwater acknowledged Sonia's comment with a faint smile. He put a foot on the bottom of the porch railing and looked out over his small orchard. Apricots, peaches, cherries, pears, oranges, and lemons—enough fruit to keep the Hacienda in pies and jams year-round. On the other side of a grove of pine trees were the vegetable gardens, and in a small pasture beyond that were a few head of dairy cattle.

"You run it very efficiently," said Dewey kindly. She really was quite impressed with the place.

"Enough to keep our table well supplied all year," Gerald replied. "Did you know we have a cheese-making operation? In a little house about two miles down the main road, at the other end of the property. A regular little dairy, complete with churns."

"Such self-sufficiency! You seem to have thought of everything."

Sonia smiled at her husband. "It's far too smelly a job for my taste, but Gerald positively shines at cheese making. He even took a course in Soft Cheeses."

"By producing most of what we need, we keep our operating costs way down," said Gerald. His gaze was still fixed on the apricot orchard beyond the front lawn. "It works out pretty well, as long as we can charge top dollar. But that's only possible with a certain clientele."

"Which we've worked hard to develop, Dewey," added Sonia. "Without those people, the taxes alone would put us on the auction block."

"Or worse," muttered Gerald.

"What would be worse?" asked Dewey.

"We have a standing offer to buy, for a fairly reasonable price."

"That's bad?"

"From someone who wants to tear down the house and the chapel, and put in condos."

"Oh." Dewey understood what a curse such an odious resolution would be. No, it probably wasn't easy on Gerald to have his home filled with paying guests all the time. But at least they were *his* guests. At least he could still invite them to sit down to dinner, show them around the property, take them to the wine cellar beneath the dining room. And of course he retained the absolute right to ask people to leave if they fell below his standards. He was still very much the master of Los Lobos. "And this person is just waiting with bated breath for you to sell? To be first in line with an offer?" It was a reasonable guess.

"That's right," said Sonia. "Not that, if it came to it, we'd be able to pick and choose. Los Lobos is huge and not very practical, really." Her eyes were suddenly filled with fear. "Someone is out to get us, Dewey. There is a vicious method to it all."

"I don't see that," Dewey objected, with a glance toward Gerald Clearwater. Apparently he agreed with his wife; he continued to stare off toward the orchard, but now he was nodding thoughtfully.

Sonia took a deep breath. "Really, Dewey, Gerald and I went through a terrible time when Monica Toro died. We were quite fond of her, both of us. And on top of that, there were all kinds of dreadful rumors circulating. Dreadful. And now, of course, everyone is willing to dig it all up again."

Dewey nodded. This was exactly what she and George had been afraid of. Someone was capitalizing on the doubts that had once been cast on the girl's death. "And somehow the staff has got hold of a rumor of the girl's ghost, or something."

Sonia contemplated her hands. "Not just the staff."

"What do you mean?"

Gerald finally pried his attention from the trees beyond. "What she means, Dewey, is that Sheriff Tate was here last week. He'd had an anonymous letter, suggesting that he reopen the investigation. On the strength of it, he came out here and showed it to us the other day."

"And?" Suddenly Dewey had a dreadful feeling in the pit of her stomach. "Surely after all this time they aren't going to come after you again. The case was closed."

Gerald Clearwater shook his head. "After each one of these little practical jokes, we have received a strange little message. I'd like your opinion." He seemed to be speaking reluctantly, making a decision. He reached inside the breast pocket of his jacket and produced a small sheaf of papers. "Here. Read these."

Dewey leafed quickly through the small pile. There wasn't much to read—they were brief messages. "Monica was here," read one. "Love from Monica," read another. There were eight or ten of them, all in the same vein. At the bottom of each one was a drawing of a skull and crossbones.

Dewey gave Sonia a stern look. "You should report these to the police."

Sonia looked pained. "That's just it, Dewey. We can't bear to do that. The sheriff somehow got wind of some of the story, and he came by here the other day, asking questions. But we couldn't tell him about the notes. If word of this got out, it would ruin us."

"So will keeping on like this."

"No. You have to help us. That's all there is to it. You have to use that famous detective ability of yours, and get to the bottom of it. And save us."

4

AFTER HER CONVERSATION with Gerald and Sonia, Dewey headed for the stables. She and George were planning to ride this morning, out across the pastureland and up the trails on the dry hillsides. But first Dewey thought she might like to have a closer look at the stables, their occupants, and most especially their manager.

The stable block was similar to the main building of the Hacienda—a large, C-shaped structure built around a central courtyard. At the center, in place of the magnolia and terrace furniture, there were bales of hay, tack, and, at the far end, a small smithy. There were more than forty stalls, but at a quick glance Dewey judged there were only about twenty horses altogether. She went as far as the office, a small room at the near end, and knocked.

"What is it?" Charles Halifax looked up from his desk. "Oh," he added, his voice overlaid with silkiness. "A guest. Do come in."

"I certainly hope I'm not disturbing you," said Dewey energetically, "but I was wondering if you might have a moment to show me around. I do so like horses, and I've heard that yours are particularly nice." She ignored Halifax's faintly concealed expression of boredom and smiled hopefully.

He waved a hand vaguely at the papers on his desk. "I'm a little busy this morning. Of course, you're welcome to look around. Help yourself." It was clear from his manner that he wasn't planning to give anyone a guided tour. He turned his attention once more to a document in his hand. It looked to Dewey like a contract of some sort.

But Dewey was not one to be put off so easily—and besides, she had a mission.

"Before I take a look around," she said, "perhaps you can give me some background. I understand your horses are quite different from the type we're accustomed to in Hamilton." Dewey made herself comfortable in the visitor's chair and prepared to be strong. It might take some doing to get this oaf to talk.

Halifax sighed. He would have to be polite, that much was the rule—guests were guests. He launched into his boilerplate about the Los Lobos stables.

"It's an interesting breed of horse," he said. "They're called Aculeo. First cousins of the Lippizaners. The Aculeo originally came over with the Spaniards, about three centuries ago. Well, of course the Spaniards were the ones who introduced horses to the New World."

He went on to explain how, in most places where they had been introduced, the breed had before long bred indiscriminately with others; in just a few isolated areas was it maintained according to the ancient bloodlines. Los Lobos was one such place; Gerald Clearwater owned the finest Aculeo breeding stable in North America, and he exported a fair number of yearlings to stables in France and Brazil, where the breed did remarkably well in certain racing classes.

Dewey expressed her enthusiasm, which fortunately she didn't have to simulate. She really did love horses, most particularly her own sweet old mare, Starbuck. She wondered briefly if Starbuck missed her. Probably. She brought her mind back to her task.

"What a wonderful job to have," she said. "And such a

beautiful setting. I would think, really, that you must feel very lucky to work at Los Lobos."

"I suppose so."

"And the rest of the staff seem *so* nice. What a pleasure to have agreeable workmates."

"Yup," Halifax said noncommittally. It was time for this old biddy to leave.

"Of course, it must have been terrible for all of you last month, when that poor girl drowned."

Halifax looked up sharply. Everybody mentioned it, sooner or later. These people just couldn't get enough of the grisly event. "I hardly knew her, actually. It's pretty easy to stay out of other people's way around here."

"Yes, I can imagine," said Dewey. "But still—perhaps people were more upset than they let on."

"I think one person was disturbed by it." Halifax looked Dewey straight in the eye. "Or haven't you heard?"

"Heard what?"

"About our ghost."

"Mercy me. A ghost?" Dewey gave an impressive shiver. "No, I haven't heard about it. Although I imagine this place has lots of them, all things considered. Is it her ghost?"

"We're supposed to think so."

"Do you believe it?"

Halifax paused a moment before replying. "I can imagine that she might not be resting easily," he said at last, in a quiet voice. As he spoke, a strange light flickered and vanished in his eyes. It came and went so quickly that Dewey wondered if she had imagined it.

"Now, Mrs.—er—"

"James. Dewey James."

"Right. Mrs. James, if you'll forgive me, I'm afraid I'm rather busy this morning." He poked at the document in his hand. "Paperwork."

"Dear me, I didn't know that there was so much paper-work at a dude ranch." She rose. "What do you do for vacation, Mr. Halifax?"

"Excuse me?"

"Well, you see—I mean, if you work in a place where others vacation, where do you vacation? Unless you don't mind having a busman's holiday, as they call it. If you follow me. Or perhaps," she added, noting his quizzical expression, "you don't need a vacation, because you work here."

"Oh, no. I get away." He had had enough of this lady, guest or no guest.

Dewey opened her eyes wide and adopted an air of understanding. "Well, of course, I know that any job has its pros and cons. Even my own job, humble as it is, has its difficult moments." Halifax, clearly uninterested, made no answer; Dewey, unperturbed, plunged ahead. "I'm a librarian, you see. Well, I'm really semiretired these days. But you might say that horses have always been a hobby of mine. They're hard to avoid, really, in my part of the world. Do you know Hamilton?"

"Been there once or twice," admitted Halifax. "I know a few of the breeders there."

"Well, I certainly hope you'll drop into the library next time you visit. I would love to show you our collection."

"Sure, sure." Halifax had had enough. "Uh, Mrs. Um—"

"James."

"Mrs. James."

"I know how stable managers can be," Dewey said, finally preparing to depart, "and believe me, if I were in charge of such a place I would be rather particular myself. So I won't take it as an offense if you'd rather I didn't go poking around all by myself."

It was clear from Halifax's expression that he didn't

really see what kind of trouble the old lady could make for him—other than be a pest the rest of his days. He rose from his desk and stepped outside to summon one of the grooms, a short, dark-haired, black-eyed man of at least seventy-five or eighty.

"Carlitos," said Halifax, in a shout, "Mrs. James would like to see the horses."

Carlitos nodded slowly and beckoned Dewey to follow him. This she did, having had the chance to study, albeit briefly, the papers on Halifax's desk. What she saw interested her.

Under Carlitos's guidance, Dewey made a tour of the stables, saying hello to the occupants politely and scratching them upon the nose or along their soft, silky cheeks. They were sweet horses, not skittish or aloof like many of the Thoroughbreds she had known; they were small and gentle and sociable. They had simple names—Honey, Buddy Boy, Azúcar, Cerveza, Soda Pop, and Pumpkin Pie.

Carlitos evidently loved to talk. He told Dewey—in English that was remarkably fluent—about the old days at Los Lobos. Carlitos had been born here, in the days of Gerald's grandfather, when the place had still been just a working ranch. He had clear memories of those days. By the time he and Dewey reached Monkey Boy, the last horse in the stable, Dewey felt she had a true picture of how the place had grown and changed over sixty years.

"Now you know how it was, before these days," he said, gesturing vaguely toward the main buildings.

"You mean, when Los Lobos was a hacienda, and not a hotel?"

Carlitos nodded, smiling. "Before these days."

"How do you feel about the conversion? Is it difficult for you, seeing your hacienda converted into a guest ranch?"

He shrugged. "I don't like it so much, but *por lo menos*

it is still here, Los Lobos. So many of the other haciendas are gone."

Dewey tried to imagine what the country must have been like seventy years ago, with three or four huge working ranches claiming most of the decent land. She asked Carlitos a few more questions. He had a remarkable memory; Dewey was certain he could tell some fascinating tales about the place, and he seemed, even now, to take a lively interest in the comings and goings of the guests.

"I like it when they come more than once," he said shyly. "Because then I know they love Los Lobos."

"Do people come back often?"

"Oh, yes." He nodded. "I see many familiar faces." He smiled. "And I never forget a face. Now, señora, if you permit me, I will choose a horse that you will like very much to ride."

He grinned and made his way to a box marked "Mal Genio."

Dewey had a little bit of Spanish, just enough to know that she'd be riding an unfamiliar horse whose name meant "Ill-tempered."

"Are you certain you want me on this one?" she asked politely.

"Oh, yes. I am sure that you are an even better rider than the other señora who is with us. She is skilled, but I am sure you are excellent."

And so it was that half an hour later, Dewey found herself astride the unfamiliar chestnut mare, admiring the equally unfamiliar landscape before her. George had arrived just in time to saddle up with her, and the two of them had left the Hacienda shortly afterwards, in company with Carlitos.

Dewey and Carlitos reached the top of a hill; he pointed the way home and explained that he would leave her and

George to find their own way back. Dewey nodded her agreement; she wanted to talk to George alone, let him know what she had learned this morning.

She adjusted her straw hat and watched as Carlitos turned his horse and headed quickly down the slope, his wide-brimmed hat flopping as he rode. On this scorched hillside, with its dry brown grass and scrubby shrubs, the sun's rays were formidable, seeming to bear down with an intense physical weight. She waited impatiently for George to catch up with her. He was carrying their canteen, which Dewey thought unnecessarily chivalrous of him; it would be nice to have it within reach. She didn't comment, however, electing not to disturb George's precarious equitational equilibrium. Unlike Dewey, who loved to ride, George was at best a reluctant horseman, and this afternoon he had already been stuck by an acacia thorn and had nearly lost his seat on a steep descent. But he remained cheerful.

She studied the scene before her with untiring interest—the white blooms on the saguaro, the pleasing dusty-green of the acacias, the pale china-blue sky without a cloud. Despite the unaccustomed heat, she liked the Escondida Valley. It was a far cry from the rolling green countryside surrounding her little hometown of Hamilton.

Dewey James was the kind of person who ordinarily didn't venture far afield to find excitement—the limitations of her pocketbook were offset by a truly adventurous mind, and she tended to bring excitement with her, or to stir it up, wherever she might be. For most of her sixty-odd years she had vacationed within two hundred miles of Hamilton. She and her late husband, Brendan, had liked to camp near Palmer Lake, when he could escape his duties as chief of the local police force, and she, hers, as the genius and the driving force behind the Hamilton Public Library. There had been a few far-flung trips—a voyage to Bermuda for their thirtieth wedding anniversary, and one or two trips to Paris, ages ago. As a young girl she had ventured once to London. But mostly she had been content to stay near home. Only fools, however, thought her life a dull one. In Hamilton, she was something of a legend, and like most small-town legends, the subject of much debate.

Unbeknownst to Dewey, her departure for Los Lobos with George Farnham had caused quite a stir in Hamilton. It was no secret that the widower Farnham dined regularly with the widow Dewey James, although Doris Bock, proprietress of the local beauty parlor and dispenser of facts great and small, was ready to swear that the romance was all on George's side. There were others who disagreed, notably Dewey's good friend Susan Miles, who possessed a great sense of what was possible in life. Susan thought that a trip together was just what Dewey needed to fall headlong into George's waiting arms. And down at the Seven Locks Tavern on the Boone River, Nils Reichart (who was ordinarily not a betting man) was taking three-to-one odds that an engagement would result.

Dewey and George, however, were cheerfully ignorant of this speculation; and if their trip had generated excitement, it was bound to be (thought Dewey) because of their destination. Even in Hamilton, people had heard of Los Lobos; Tom Campbell, a pompous and ignorant stuffed shirt who worked with Dewey at the library, claimed to know people who had friends who were regular visitors to the famed Hacienda. (But then, Tom Campbell *would* make such a claim, Dewey thought. He was just like Mr. Collins in *Pride and Prejudice*.)

Certainly Dewey had never vacationed in a place so full of indulgence, luxury, and all the trappings of money. She rather liked the feeling it gave her to choose from among four types of bath oils in a marble-clad bathroom with antique brass fixtures, to have people attending to her needs from morning till night, to have two chocolates on her pillow at bedtime. It was all extremely novel and—despite Dewey's strong streak of common sense—appealing.

Now, as she gazed down in the direction of the Hacienda Los Lobos, a mile or so up the little valley, Dewey wondered again how she would cope with the intriguing problem before her. The notes that Gerald and Sonia had shown her could be classified either as spooky or sinister. She wasn't sure how she felt about them. Charles Halifax had seemed oddly anxious about the whole situation, but perhaps Dewey mistook mere irritation for anxiety. He had seemed almost to believe in the ghost story, although he hardly seemed the type to fall for tales of the supernatural.

She came out of her reverie and looked around her once more, as George, at long last, reached the crest of the hill. The desert spread out before her in a beautiful panorama of browns and subtle gray-greens, their colors receding as the sun rose higher in the sky.

Far below she could make out the buildings of the Hacienda—a group of one-story stucco buildings around a central courtyard, with the small adobe chapel off toward the north, and a tennis court and swimming pool to the south. Near the start of the hillside riding trail were the stables. These, like most of Los Lobos, dated from the period of the Spanish settlement of the valley.

"Whoa, Nellie," George said to his horse, as he finally drew up beside Dewey. He looked around for Carlitos. "Did our fearless leader desert us?"

"Not exactly. We just take this path straight down to get home." Dewey pointed in front of them. "Carlitos says it's easy."

"Easy for you and Carlitos, maybe," returned George, but Dewey could tell that he didn't mind too much. He grinned at her. "At least I had a good morning. Made friends with the chef. He says I can spend as much time as I want in the kitchen, since it's a slow week."

"How nice for you, George," Dewey said distractedly. In Hamilton, George was known for his gourmet cooking skills, while his good friend Dewey was famous for knowing next to nothing about how to cook. She loved to eat, but she had little patience for the things that happened before you sat down at the table.

George noted her distraction with a smile and changed the subject. "Well? What about your famous mission? Tell me all about your top secret conference this morning."

Dewey sighed. "I hope Sonia and Gerald's confidence in me isn't misplaced. So far, I have drawn a complete blank. But do you know, George, something is definitely up. I feel sorry for Sonia."

"How so?"

Dewey explained about the notes from "Monica."

"They should go to the police." George was succinct. Dewey studied his face and wondered again about his decision to come with her. If he had come to protect her from a ghost, it looked like he would find himself pitted against something more substantial—and more malicious.

"That's what I told them, but it seems they're taking the stubborn route. They're terribly worried about their clientele."

"I can see why they might feel that way," George admitted.

"I think they have two problems, really," Dewey said thoughtfully. "The first is that they have to clear up the story about that young woman's death. There must be something unresolved, if after the case was closed last month the sheriff is willing to look into it again. Then they can worry about the ghost."

"Her drowning wasn't exactly good for business, I would guess."

"Probably not," Dewey agreed. "In spite of all their efforts to keep it quiet, they may still get unwanted publicity." She told George about the anonymous letter that had been sent to the county sheriff. "He came out here the other day to tell them about it."

"And scared them to death, no doubt."

"No doubt," agreed Dewey.

The two old friends sat side by side, looking out at the majestic landscape before them.

"The appearance of these notes puts quite a different spin on things, George. Things are seldom what they seem."

George Farnham was used to Dewey's elliptical way of talking, and merely nodded.

"And you'll have to admit," she went on, "that you were quite wrong about the ghost." She reached into her shirt pocket and produced one of Monica's notes. "This was written by someone of flesh and blood."

George took the note and looked at it curiously. It did seem as though someone were trying to put a scare into the guests at Los Lobos. But why?

Dewey read his mind. "Sonia thinks that someone's trying to drive them out of business."

"Mmm."

"It's not all that farfetched, George. People are scared of ghosts and mysteries—most people, anyway. They're fine in a movie, but not here in real life."

"But there isn't a ghost. I thought you were sure of that."

"I am," replied Dewey. "But I'm equally sure that somebody or something is strange around this place. And I think we should find out what it is."

"Find out what what is?" came a booming voice from above them.

Dewey and George both jumped. They looked quickly around for the source, and finally spotted Charles Halifax, seated on a boulder about ten yards away.

There was no telling how long he'd been there.

"Find out what what is?" he asked again, merely swinging his fat legs and grinning down at George and Dewey.

5

THE BRAND-NEW ATHLETIC facilities at Los Lobos were beautifully outfitted with all the latest in gym equipment. There was nothing lacking; Gerald and Sonia had seen to it that Monica Toro had got everything she wanted. Hers was a dream spa, replete with resistance equipment, massage tables, automatic sit-up tables, Jacuzzis and saunas and a steam room, mud baths, nutritional counseling, and even a juice bar. Alas and alack, Monica Toro was no longer able to preside over her domain.

Since Monica's death, Harriet Bray had done her earnest best to attract guests to the gym. Perhaps because of her earnestness, however—or perhaps because of lingering sensations of discomfort associated with Monica's death—the guests didn't go near the place, as a rule. Harriet was becoming more and more frustrated; shut out by Charles from the job she was supposed to have, she was obliged to interest people in something they had no use for. Every time she went near the gym, she felt more aggravated, useless, and depressed.

Perhaps it was these very qualities, however, that attracted the Miltons to Harriet. Either that, or the fact that they didn't like to ride, and really weren't very well suited to enjoying the beauty of the landscape or the company of the other guests at the Hacienda. Dewey and George were off on horseback; the nature photographers had gone in search of ant-lions; Eloise Morningside was playing tennis with Mark Harris. The Miltons went, heavy-footed, to Harriet Bray's gym, where they announced themselves interested in physical fitness.

Harriet, enormously pleased to have a client or two, arranged a schedule for them for the week. First thing in the morning seemed to suit them. They had no inclination to linger over morning coffee with the other guests, and an early hour would spare Harriet from having to witness one more of Charles Halifax's disgusting breakfasts. She was suddenly exceeding grateful to the Miltons, and when they had gone, she turned to her stereo system with enthusiasm. She popped in her newest tape and worked for the next hour, inventing a really exciting routine. Something fun. Something worth getting up for. For the Miltons, nothing too heavy. She would advise a warm-up with music, followed by fifteen minutes of aerobics (moderately paced), capped off with a quick-and-easy ten minutes on the resistance equipment. Then a cool-down and a Jacuzzi.

When the aerobics routine was completed, she thought about the rest of the program. The resistance equipment was next. She would try to get them on the Thigh-a-lyzer.

The Thigh-a-lyzer had been Monica's pride and joy. It was a huge, grim-looking, muscle-building contraption—a chair whose makers promised that in it you could strengthen all your leg muscles at once. Harriet had used it herself only a few times, and before she put any of the guests on it, she needed to become more familiar with it. The Thigh-a-lyzer was kind of threatening, Harriet thought. It was a jungle of straps and hinges and huge black cushions, with a tall column of serious-looking weights at the back.

Now, to get ready for the Miltons, Harriet read the instructions for the machine. She carefully piled on the weights and adjusted the levers so that the machine would work on the inner thigh. (That was the place where even

Harriet Bray sometimes carried an extra gram or two of fat.)
She settled in deliberately and buckled the straps in place.
She exerted pressure with her legs, and the column of
weights came up just like they were supposed to. Then, with
a thundering crash, they cascaded to the floor. Harriet,
struggling inexpertly against the suddenly unresisting machine, was knocked off balance by her own inertia. She
struggled to stay upright, and the Thigh-a-lyzer overturned
completely, trapping poor Harriet beneath its menacing
protrusions and straps.

George and Dewey turned their horses home and rode for
the next half hour in silence. Dewey seemed lost in thought.
They had almost reached Los Lobos when George finally
spoke.

"I wonder how long he'd been listening to us," he said.
"Made me uncomfortable to see him sitting there."

"We shall never know," said Dewey. "I think he's the
kind of person who loves to eavesdrop, just because he
knows how upsetting it can be."

"Now what makes you say that?"

"Didn't you see the look on his face, George? It was a
smirk of a very superior sort. He reminds me of a boy that
used to plague me at the library. Jimmy Flood. A perfect
little demon."

"Richie Flood's little boy?"

"That's right."

"The father was a troublemaker, too. And now that you
mention it, he did have that same little smirk." Dewey was
often right about such things, George had to admit. "Well, I
guess the cat's out of the bag now. You can just go ahead
and grill people if you want, now that your cover is blown."

"I suppose so," Dewey agreed. "And I think I'll start with
Harriet Bray. After all, she and the dead woman used to

work together." They rode the rest of the way in silence, and Dewey headed toward the gym.

When she entered the gym, Dewey at first thought that there was no one there. After a moment, however, she heard a shout from the weight room, and found Harriet pinned under the grim-looking chair. The Thigh-a-lyzer was, if anything, more horrific upside down than right side up. Dewey gasped and rushed to help, unstrapping a grateful and trembling Harriet. The young woman appeared to have no broken bones, and the two of them, with effort, righted the machine. Harriet, flustered and nervous, dusted herself off and looked at Dewey with curiosity.

"Thank you, Mrs. James," she said, huffing and puffing a bit. "It's lucky you came along."

"I think you would have managed to rescue yourself in time," Dewey assured her. "Are you all right?"

"I think so. My ankle hurts."

"You'd better put some ice on it."

"I will," said Harriet. She hobbled over to Monica's little corner office, which held a small refrigerator, and took out a blue ice pack. Then she settled down on a bench and raised her foot. "If you've come to sign up for instruction, I guess this isn't the best time. I'm really not cut out for this sort of thing."

"Oh, heavens, no," replied Dewey. "As far as exercise goes, I've never been much of a one for such organized, sporty things."

"No?" Harriet looked up reprovingly. "Exercise is very, very important."

"So they say." Out of the corner of her eye Dewey spotted a small slip of paper, trapped underneath one of the weights that had fallen off the Thigh-a-lyzer. She inched toward it. "Of course, I love to walk and ride."

"Well, I'm glad to hear that. As long as you get plenty of

moderate exercise every day, that's really all that counts."
Harriet frowned at her ankle.

"Oh, I do," Dewey said in a soothing voice. Harriet Bray
seemed really concerned. Dewey wanted to relieve her
mind. "But I'm afraid I'm inclined to be independent. I'm
far more comfortable on my own." She bent and began to
pick up the fallen weights.

"Don't do that, Mrs. James."

"Oh, I don't mind a bit," replied Dewey, stacking the
weights in a neat pile. She picked up the piece of paper and
slid it quickly into a pocket. "I really just came to have a
look around, and I like to be helpful, you know." She gave
Harriet an innocent look. "We haven't got a facility like this
in Hamilton. So I thought I'd just take a look. All the girls
back home will want to hear about it."

"Sure." Harriet hobbled to her feet. "Let me give you the
tour."

"But your ankle—"

"It will be fine, Mrs. James. Really."

Harriet insisted, and Dewey—with practiced reluctance—
allowed the young woman to give her the full tour. Luckily,
Dewey had nothing particular to do with the rest of her
morning; clearly, Harriet Bray liked to talk. By the end of
half an hour, Dewey felt that she knew everything there was
to know about resistance equipment, its design, and the
safest and most effective manner of using it. Finally, she
spotted a break, and she dove in.

"My, it's quite a facility," remarked Dewey, as they were
completing their circuit of the indoor swimming pool. "It
must be a tremendous job for one person. I think you should
have an assistant."

"Oh." Harriet gave Dewey a curious look. "Well, there
used to be another person here, actually. The truth is, I'm

Charles Halifax's assistant at the stables. I'm just filling in at the gym for now."

"Oh? You mean there's someone else?"

"Well, um, there used to be." Harriet led the way to the sauna and opened the door. "Personally, I prefer sauna to steam heat, because it's much healthier. But we offer both, of course."

"I'm partial to steam myself," lied Dewey, who thought them both barbaric and uncomfortable. "Did she leave, the other woman?"

"Yes." Harriet looked oddly at Dewey. "Don't you know about this?"

"About what?"

"I thought everybody knew. I mean, it was in the paper and everything. Don't you know about Monica?"

"No. She used to work here with you? Did something happen to her?"

"Well, yes." Harriet frowned. "She drowned, last month."

"Oh, dear heavens, how dreadful," Dewey said, automatically. "That must have been a terrible shock."

"It was. Especially because she was a really good swimmer."

"Oh—well, now, even great swimmers can drown."

"I suppose." Harriet led the way to the squash courts. "These are new," she said, opening one of the tiny doors for Dewey to peer through. "They're state-of-the-art. Of course we have graphite racquets for our guests to use, and you can play soft ball or hard ball."

"Very nice," Dewey said admiringly. She hadn't the faintest idea how to play squash, but she thought the little door to the court was sort of cute. "It happened here, in your pool?"

"Yes." Harriet shut the small door with a thud and gave

the handle a twist. "I was thinking yesterday that Monica would really have loved to meet Eloise Morningside."

"She is rather glamorous, isn't she?"

"I'll say. Monica just adored *Faces*, too. She used to write fan letters to the magazine."

"A great number of people do enjoy it," Dewey said evenly. She wasn't a fan, herself.

"She must have written them a lot, too, because sometimes they wrote her back. She saved every one."

They had come out through a side door into the fore court of the gymnasium building. They had made the full tour. Harriet gestured to a small wooden bench under a tall palm tree, and the two of them sat down. Harriet stretched her right leg out before her and examined her ankle, which had swollen hugely.

She turned her glance from her swollen ankle to Dewey. "You know, Mrs. James, I told Gerald, but he thought I was just being too imaginative or something. But I don't think they ever really looked into it all that carefully."

"Monica's death?"

"Yeah. It was really weird that she would go swimming at night. Especially that night."

"Why was it weird?"

"Well, it was late. It was after dinner, anyway. Must have been past eight o'clock."

"And that was unusual for her?"

"Yup. She swam every morning, but not at night. Not usually."

Dewey considered this for a moment. Sonia and Gerald had told her that Harriet had only begun working with them in March. Her knowledge of what was usual would be based on one month's acquaintance with the dead girl and might not be very accurate at all.

"I mean, it was really weird," Harriet went on, "because

I had the feeling, you know, like a premonition, that she was heading for some kind of trouble."

"How do you mean?"

"Well, she was all excited about something. She wouldn't tell me about it—well, she said she would, someday. She only said she was going to be set for life."

"Oh, dear," said Dewey. To her, such a claim often sounded either foolhardy or deluded.

"Anyway, it was Rodeo Week in Edmunds, and there were all kinds of things going on, and there were just two couples at the Hacienda, older people who were really boring and didn't really want to do anything much." Harriet blushed suddenly, but Dewey helped her over her faux pas.

"That's quite all right, my dear. You haven't hurt my feelings."

"Sorry. Anyway, so we went into town every night that week, because Rodeo Week is kind of one long party. And then the last night, I went to get her in our room."

"You were her roommate?"

"Oh, yeah. All the whole month, but we were supposed to get separate rooms in April. Anyway, she wasn't there. So I thought maybe she'd already gotten a lift down to Edmunds, maybe with Mark or Sidney, or even with Charles. He used to be pretty nice to Monica, even though he hates just about everybody."

"That must make it nice to be his assistant."

Harriet rolled her eyes. "If I didn't love horses so much—Well, anyway, I didn't see Monica so I just went down to town. And I didn't see her down there, and then the next day nobody could find her. Until they found her."

"How terribly sad."

"I spent that whole night worried that something had happened to her. It was weird. And now—well, now it's all even weirder. They all say she's coming back to haunt us."

Harriet looked at her ankle. "They're going to say it was her ghost again."

"What do you mean? What was her ghost?"

"The machine in there, the one that fell over with me in it. That was rigged up, Mrs. James. We have somebody playing tricks. But then everybody thinks it's Monica, that she's dead and her ghost is getting back at us all here, or trying to get our attention, or something."

"You don't believe in ghosts, do you, Harriet?"

"Well, I don't know. I never used to believe in excellent swimmers just drowning all of a sudden, either. Now I sort of don't know what to think." She gave Dewey a smile. "Look at me. I'm supposed to be such an expert in physical fitness, and I sprain my own ankle. I'd better go stick some more ice on it, Mrs. James. If Gerald and Sonia find out, they might think I'm no good for what's left of my job."

"Yes, indeed," Dewey replied thoughtfully. Harriet hobbled off and Dewey withdrew from her shirt pocket the slip of paper that she had retrieved.

"Greetings from Monica," it read.

Dewey carefully put it back in her pocket and went off to find George Farnham.

6

DINNER AT THE Hacienda Los Lobos was always an experience. For most people, the charm that Gerald and Sonia exerted was the main reason for coming back to stay again and again; the Clearwaters had the knack of making their audience feel that they were the only people who had ever been lucky enough to be invited to spend a night with them at the family estate. It was this charm, more than anything else, that guaranteed the Hacienda's "Royale" rating among hotels, and which made the sky-high daily tariffs seem reasonable. Indeed, Dewey imagined that most of the paying guests at Los Lobos forgot, while they were there, that there would be a bill coming due at the end of their stay. The Clearwaters had that effect on people.

Gerald was often extremely witty on the subject of his eccentric ancestors, who had grown rich through many an unorthodox practice, and who had stayed rich right up until the Great Depression, when Gerald's grandfather—apparently the first honest member of the family—had lost most of the family fortune. All that he had retained had been the Los Lobos property, which at the time had been severely undervalued by the local tax authorities. It had been Grandfather's only lucky break.

Gerald's stories were full of references to pirate ships and kidnappers, to buried treasure, stolen cattle, and the hunt for gold in mountain streams. One of his favorite subjects was his great-grandmother, who had trained ferrets for a hobby.

As a young woman, she had scandalized her family and the neighborhood by seizing the pulpit of the family chapel one Sunday morning and preaching a fiery and impromptu sermon on the evils of the inequality of the sexes.

Gerald's tales all had a fresh air about them; if Dewey hadn't known him and Sonia so well, she would never have suspected that they had told the same stories at least a hundred times to an assemblage of quests.

Tonight was no exception. Generally, guests who came to Los Lobos stayed for a week or so, arriving on a Sunday and leaving the following Saturday. The first night around the big dining room table was often awkward; people unused to formal dining in a family setting worried that they might pick up the wrong fork or otherwise betray their inelegance. Sonia and Gerald generally used the first night for taking the measure of their new guests, discovering what they liked to talk about, what was likely to offend them, and what the group dynamics would be like.

In this case, it had taken them about five minutes to size up the group. Dewey and George, of course, were known quantities. Lorenzo and Serena apparently were full of unbounded enthusiasm for insect life, but little else. Eloise Morningside liked to talk about Eloise Morningside. She had a real gift for making people think she was talking about something or someone else, but the subject rarely varied. The Miltons clearly didn't have a subject.

As a whole, the group was worse than awful, dragged down by the deadweight of the uncooperative Miltons. With couples, there was often some kind of tension; if this was the case, the Clearwaters would divide and conquer, Sonia winning over the men and Gerald the women, so that by the end of their stay, both people felt attractive, charming, and altogether delightful. It was an obvious technique, but it had helped to smooth over the rough spots in many marriages.

The Miltons were different, however. They were united in their unwillingness, joined in their lack of jollity. Even hosts as experienced as Sonia and Gerald knew that there wasn't much you could do with two oafs who were determined not to enjoy themselves. The Miltons would simply have to lump it.

Sonia and Gerald adjusted their technique. The conversation on the second evening became quite general, requiring only as much participation as everyone wished to give. Belinda Milton sat on Gerald's right, and Philip Milton on Sonia's left; thus divided, they could do less damage with their sour looks, and they could be skillfully encouraged should they show the least sign of wishing to participate in the festivities.

Sonia turned to George, who was on her right, and began to discuss food, which was always a good topic. The Miltons were silent. Serena and Lorenzo babbled cheerfully about Nature to whoever would listen—to each other, that is to say.

Dewey, finding herself next to Eloise Morningside, knew what to talk about.

"And how are you enjoying Los Lobos so far?" she asked.

"I think it's marvelous. Simply marvelous," Eloise gushed. "You know, it's the kind of place where you find repose— so necessary, I can tell you, if your life is a hectic one." She gave Dewey a sympathetic look whose meaning was clear: Dewey did not lead a hectic life, and would probably never know, poor thing, what it was to be busy and important.

Dewey ignored the look. She was generally indifferent to such slights—and generally too busy to worry about being important. "Yes, I suppose this must be quite different from your life in New York."

"Quite." She sized Dewey up. "Have you ever been to New York?"

It seemed to Dewey that Eloise stopped short—that she had meant to say "Have you ever been to New York, you hayseed?" But Dewey smiled and nodded. "Several times, in fact," she enthused, hoping that she sounded wide-eyed and provincial. Hoo-hoo! Several times! What a treat for the hayseed!

Eloise smirked. "Well, as a visitor of course you don't really get to know the city. It's only when you've become part of the fabric of the Metropolis that you can understand the difference between that universe and all the rest."

"Undoubtedly," agreed Dewey. What planet was that? "And of course, as the editor of *Faces* you're probably much busier than most of us." Did people really believe that of themselves? "But I guess you meet hundreds of exciting people—so it must be enjoyable work."

Eloise's expression changed to one of superior wariness. Now the hayseed was going to ask about Celebrities. What a bore. "Naturally. Well, it's probably hard to imagine how busy one gets."

Dewey played along, nodding. Predictably, Eloise shifted the topic. "In fact, this is really my first trip to this part of the world. I don't get away much from my desk, as a rule." She gave Dewey a look. "Do you work?"

"Oh, my heavens, yes. I'm a librarian."

"Oh?" Eloise reached for the salt.

"That is to say, I'm semiretired, really, at this point. But we have quite a nice little library in Hamilton, and I pride myself on our collection."

"I'm not much of a reader, myself. I really don't have the time for it." With that Eloise turned to Gerald, who was in the middle of a tale about his great-grandmother, who had died a rather unexpected death at a young age. Her husband had then remarried the daughter of one of the ranch hands; fortunately for Gerald, there had been no children from that marriage.

"So my grandmother Torcaza was the sole heir, when my great-grandfather died. She was quite lucky, because she could just as easily have had six or seven half brothers and sisters to share the place with."

"She was an only child?" asked Dewey.

"That's right. It was quite unusual, in those days; and of course she was *quite* rich, and much sought after. I've heard that men she had never met wrote her letters proposing marriage. And she was always receiving anonymous love letters."

"Speaking of anonymous letters," put in Serena Lee, "I hear that you've been having a plague of them." She looked around at the group, who had all been surprised into silence.

Sonia, ever composed, was the first to speak. "I really wouldn't give that story a moment's thought," she said. She reached for the small brass bell in the center of the table and rang for the servants, who appeared silently and surefootedly to clear the soup bowls and bring up the main course—rosemary-stuffed zucchini and grilled lamb chops.

"But from what I hear, this is indeed more than a story," insisted Serena, taking three lamb chops and suddenly becoming interested in the conversation. "Pah—everybody knows all about it, that is the way with such things. It's true, isn't it, that there have been many strange occurrences lately at Los Lobos. Although, as a scientist, I do not subscribe to supernatural theories."

"I think," inserted Gerald, sounding to Dewey's ears a trifle anxious, "that maybe the whole thing has been blown way out of proportion." He gave a practiced shrug of his shoulders. "It's really not worth thinking about—and I'd advise you to ignore any rumors you've heard."

"What's all this?" asked Eloise. She turned to George, who was seated next to her. "I heard the magic word—*rumor!*" She giggled. "It's important to know when there's a story brewing," she said musically, waving her fingertips in the direction of their hostess. "Come, Sonia. Is it something that would interest *Faces*? Believe it or not, I was a cub reporter once." Eloise evidently found the image of herself as a mere reporter extremely amusing; she burst into mirthful laughter, which the group clearly was meant to share. Such was the power of her personality that they all did chuckle politely. "Tell," she insisted.

Gerald had utterly regained his composure and struggled to take control of the conversation once more. He stepped in smoothly, the fabled raconteur of Los Lobos. "This is the kind of place, Eloise," he said, with a twinkle in his blue eyes, "that sparks fantasy from time to time. Over the centuries, there have been all kinds of crazy stories about ghosts. My great-uncle Horacio used to make up stories like that, to keep people away. He was a terrible misanthrope."

"But we're not talking about something in the past, but the present, no?" asked Serena. She snapped her fingers. "Today, from my chambermaid, I learned that your entire staff thinks you have a ghost here."

"We don't have a ghost," Sonia insisted matter-of-factly. Her face was stony; Dewey could tell that she was quickly calculating which staff member served as Serena's chambermaid. No doubt there would be a few words on the subject tomorrow morning.

"I've often wondered if, according to the law of conservation of energy and matter, our spirits do persist beyond our lifetimes," said Lorenzo. They all looked at him.

"So you believe in ghosts?" asked Belinda Milton, sounding skeptical. "I thought you were a scientist."

It was hard to read the expression on his face; he glanced

nervously toward Serena, as if half-expecting her to shut him up. But she seemed as intrigued as everyone else. It was an unexpected philosophy in an insect man, and it seemed to be news to her. He cleared his throat and explained further. "You see, if things that exist have to go on existing, which they do, then the energy that comprises our spirits—for want of a more scientific word—should by rights go on existing even after our deaths."

"So everything has a ghost. Even insects?" Philip Milton's voice was taunting. "Or do we make an exception?"

"Well, they must," said George, "if we're defining spirit as the energy that attaches to a living creature."

"Is the spirit then the same thing as the soul?" asked Eloise. She directed her question at George, but it was Serena who replied.

"I would imagine that depends on one's conscience," she said. "Certain Hindus, for example, believe in the spirit of all living things. Isn't that correct, Lorenzo?"

"Yes, indeed, my dear."

"But if an insect has a soul, then it has to have free will," insisted Belinda Milton. "How many ants do you know with free will?"

"No, you're all wrong," said Serena rudely. "That would be true only if you accept a certain limited and very traditional, Western definition of a soul. Anyhow, we are off the subject." She glared at Lorenzo. He was the one who had started all of this, with his nonsense about spirits. Then she turned her glare on Sonia. "You haven't answered our question. What is all this about a ghost? Is it true that someone was murdered here?"

7

THAT EVENING, WHILE the diners at Los Lobos were discussing free will in ants, Larry Ceboll had been surveying his work with particular self-congratulation. The *Foothill Trumpeter* might be a small paper, but it reached every important person in Edmunds, Villaseca, and all of Lincoln County. Plus, where else in the world could you print whatever you wanted about people you didn't like?

"Larry, I think you've gone too far," Julia Ceboll, Larry's bossy wife, had commented. She held up this week's *Trumpeter.*

On page one, over a photo of the famous ranch house, the headline read: TRAGIC DEATH STILL HAUNTS HACIENDA. The article ("Special to the *Trumpeter,*" according to the byline) quoted from the letter to Packy Tate and described the series of strange, "ghostly" occurrences up at Los Lobos. "This might be the end of high-priced hospitality at Los Lobos," the article concluded. "Nobody likes to live with ghosts. Sheriff Packy Tate is following the not-so-sweet scent of the case, and he won't rest until he comes to the end of the trail. This community wants to be certain that we have all learned the truth about the tragic death of young Monica Toro."

Nobody could tell Larry Ceboll that he didn't treat his woman right. He took her out once a week to the Foothill Diner. Tonight, as always, the air was sonorous with the clatter of plate on plate, the shouts of the cook to the waitresses, and the constant sizzle of hamburgers on the grill. The air was rich with the aroma of old Friolator fat, homemade pies, and stale coffee. Julia and Larry both enjoyed their weekly dinners out, although they generally squabbled. They were born fighters, the both of them.

As part-owner of the *Trumpeter*, Julia reserved the right to comment on every issue. Ordinarily she didn't care much what her obnoxious husband saw fit to print, worrying only about the advertising revenues. Julia Ceboll had a very practical mind for the newspaper business. This week, however, her practical mind warned her that Larry was starting up one of his campaigns against the Clearwaters. It was dangerous; the Clearwaters were powerful people, even if they weren't as rich as they used to be, and they had a lot of friends and family connections in the capital. They would pull strings if Larry got too obvious, or too obnoxious.

Julia, being not only bossier but also far more agile mentally than her heavy-handed husband, usually came out on top. Usually, but not always—there were times when Larry just could not let Julia's cooler head prevail.

"Too far," Julia said again.

"Nah." He reached across the table for the salt shaker, which was slippery with the grease of many years. He shook some on his fries. "Do 'em good."

Julia didn't share her husband's dislike of the Los Lobos family. She shook her head. "Where'd you get that business about the ghost?"

"I have my sources."

"Don't be ridiculous. I want to know."

"I'm not telling."

"Be that way. I wash my hands of it." She read through the article one more time. "They'll sue, you know."

"Big deal," replied Larry.

"If they sue, it *will* be a big deal, Larry. For you. I wash my hands of it. I refuse to bail you out of this one. You should know better."

"If they sue, they sue the paper. Not me. So you're in whether you like it or not. Besides, they aren't gonna sue."

"No? For damage to their business? For deliberately trying to scare people away? You watch out, Larry Ceboll. I'm warning you now. I know what you're up to. There isn't a person in Edmunds who won't figure it out, either. You've always been greedy. You've always been jealous of Gerald for having that ranch."

"Oh, shut up, Julia," replied Larry. He poured ketchup on his omelette. "Just shut up. I can say whatever I want about those stupid people, so just shut up."

"Who's there?" George Farnham's voice asked in the darkness. He was outside of Dewey's room, on the portico of the west wing. The other guests had gone off to bed already; the Lees and the Miltons had left the red parlor first, followed by Eloise Morningside. George, because he was such a gentleman, had seen Eloise to her room; but Dewey had stayed to talk to Sonia and Gerald. Now she was making her solitary way back from the dinner table. "Is that you, Dewey?"

"Yes, it's I," said Dewey, rather correctly. She was feeling out of sorts.

"Staying out awfully late, aren't you?" he asked her playfully.

"Am I? I didn't realize it was late. I was talking to Gerald and Sonia."

"That dinner conversation was a bit awkward, wouldn't you say?" George took a seat on the wicker settee on the portico and gestured for Dewey to join him.

"I thought Sonia and Gerald handled it rather well, all things considered." She sat down.

"It could have been worse," George agreed. "Serena missed her calling. Should have been a dentist. Good at extractions."

Dewey agreed. Serena had been excellent at getting the stubborn Clearwaters to tell their story to the guests. In the face of her inelegant persistence, they finally had little choice but to discuss, as briefly as possible, the death of Monica Toro and the series of pranks perpetrated at the Hacienda.

The scene, had it not been painful, might have been amusing. Dewey recalled how Sonia had described the little notes that they had found. Throughout, Belinda Milton's scowl had deepened, and she had finally given her husband an apologetic look, saying, "Sorry."

"What's that?" Serena had interposed sharply.

"Nothing," Philip had answered quickly—but it was too late. Serena eventually wrested from Belinda an account of an enormous misunderstanding. Belinda had found a note in the bathroom—she thought maybe it had come from Philip's toilet kit—that read "Love from Monica." Naturally enough, the little message had caused Belinda much anxiety.

"Poor Belinda," said George, chuckling at the recollection. "Thinking that Philip had some secret lover."

"Poor *Philip*," amended Dewey. "He was truly hung for a lamb." It seemed unfair to Dewey—although she imagined that marriage to Philip was no day at the beach.

"Well, now that Eloise Morningside knows, I wonder if she'll make hay of it." George sounded speculative; but whether he approved of *Faces* or not, it was difficult for Dewey to tell. A surprising number of very respectable people did like the magazine, although Dewey much preferred *Vanity Fair* and *People*. She thought *Faces* was a little dishonest—it pretended to be highfalutin, to be gossip of a higher caliber, instead of honestly admitting to being what it was. Dewey thought that hypocritical. Give her an honest scandal sheet any day. She thought she might even prefer the *Foothill Trumpeter*, the little local weekly newspaper. This morning she had seen last week's issue, and by the looks of things, the *Trumpeter* didn't pull its punches.

"I don't see why she'd bother, frankly," said Dewey. In the darkness, an owl called. There were footsteps from across the portico, on the opposite side of the courtyard, and the sound of voices floated toward them through the darkness. Dewey thought she recognized the voice of Mark Harris. The other voice was unmistakable—Harriet Bray's. Overhead, through the topmost branches of the magnolia, a full moon was shining an intense white, blotting out all the stars.

"If Sonia's worried about the publicity, she might just ask her to keep quiet about it."

"I doubt such a request would have much influence, one way or another. Don't you imagine that if Eloise thinks it's good copy, she'll write it up, full of all kinds of atmosphere and embellishments?"

"I would guess so," George agreed.

"On the other hand," Dewey said pensively, "she may well think it all a bit of a bore, when she gets back to her other universe."

"How's that?"

"Nothing," Dewey said quickly. She didn't intend to be ironical about Eloise Morningside. Life was too short. She stood, bade George good night, and headed for her room.

8

"WELL, THERE'S ONE I recognize. That's a crow," said George gamely, pointing up toward a fat black bird perched in a ponderosa pine.

"You've got me," responded Philip Milton, sounding bored. Evidently the stockbroker wasn't much of a birder. Neither was George, but he was certainly willing to make a little effort this morning.

It was Tuesday morning, and Harriet Bray—forced to cancel her aerobics class—had offered a nature walk in its place. Thanks to Charles Halifax's constant belittling remarks, she had half-expected the excursion to be sneered at as a stupid idea. Greatly to her surprise, the response had been quite positive. Everyone, in fact, had decided to tag along—nicest of all, the Lees, who were, after all, real experts. Maybe that was why the others had come, too, Harriet thought. Or maybe they all felt a little bit sorry for her. Whatever the reason, she would have the success of her nature walk to rub in Charles Halifax's fat face.

George Farnham and Philip Milton were well ahead of the rest of the group. Harriet herself was limping, with her badly sprained ankle in an Ace bandage; it evidently cost her to keep up with the men, so she walked alongside Eloise Morningside. The two of them appeared to be having an absorbing conversation, although most of the talk was on one side.

Belinda Milton walked alone. Lorenzo and Serena trailed

71

far behind, because they were constantly stopping to inspect the ground—they were searching for ant lion traps, they told Dewey. That lady, briefly fascinated by such earnest enthusiasm for bugs, stayed close to the nature experts to see what they came up with.

It was either that, Dewey reflected, or listen to one of Harriet Bray's lectures on fitness. This morning, Harriet had already regaled them with tales of the dangers of gluten and a register of her allergies—to onions and their ilk, to raisins, to chocolate, and most of all to mustard. Ingestion of this condiment, Harriet avowed, could bring on anaphylactic shock. Even death. Dewey often thought that there wasn't anything quite as dull as listening to other people talk about their dietary preferences. So, for now, she stuck with the nature photographers.

She was oddly intrigued by their all-consuming love for their chosen topic, and impressed by the apparent depth of their fascination for what seemed to her mere barren, near-desert ground. She also thought they were about the weirdest people she had ever met in her life—and Dewey had come across a few oddities in her time. This morning they busily took photographs of the scenery—which admittedly was dramatic—and lectured Dewey on their craft.

"Nature photography requires a great deal of patience, and more than a little skill," Serena told her. The matter-of-fact voice was traced with pride—Serena was not the type of woman to shrink from uttering awkward truths, complimentary to herself though they might be. "To be a great specialist—we specialize in insects—you must be a true artist. Isn't that right, Lorenzo?" she appealed to her husband.

"Yes, my dear," Lorenzo concurred. "Exactly right." He stopped briefly and adjusted the focus on his lens. Before them the valley sloped away, and in the distance could be seen the brilliant blue surface of a small lake.

"You have to be a true artist," Serena was saying, "but you also must possess the knowledge of the most learned of scientists."

"That's very true," Lorenzo added, stopping to admire a small termite mound. "Fabulous. What a life they lead."

"Indeed," Dewey had replied, not sure what to say. Was that entomology or etymology? She always confused the two. "Etymology" sounded more like insects, somehow, but she thought the word was really "entomology." She could ask, but on the whole she thought she'd prefer just guessing. Entomology, she guessed. She'd look it up when they got back to Los Lobos.

"An intimate understanding of the nature of insect life," Lorenzo went on, "is a prerequisite. Wouldn't you say so, Serena?"

"That's right." Serena nodded firmly as she stooped to investigate a small depression in the ground. "A prerequisite."

"I'm certain it must be," Dewey enthused.

"And an understanding of how insects think, how they feel. Remember that each species is different. As different as we are from, say, horses and dogs."

"Yes," said Dewey, who was remarkable for her ability to understand and get along with both horses and dogs. She didn't think they were really so different from people. "That must take a great deal of study."

"Be honest," Serena said bossily, "you find insects a little repellent, do you not?"

Dewey had to admit that she did.

"So many people do," Serena lamented. "However, we are not afraid, you see, am I, dear?" This time she didn't wait for Lorenzo's antiphonal response; her voice grew more oratorical, and she pointed at her chest with her forefinger. "I am not afraid to move right into the tarantula's lair, to sleep with the scorpion if need be. I am an artist and a scientist, at once." She held up her gesticulating forefinger. "At once."

"Yes, indeed," said Dewey, perhaps a little too heartily. She wasn't squeamish, but she couldn't really relish talk of tarantulas and scorpions.

"Lorenzo and I have traveled the globe, we have come to know every inch of wilderness that can be known. We are experts, you might say."

No, *you* might say, thought Dewey, but she merely nodded and looked politely enquiring.

"Do you know the ant lion, Mrs. James?" asked Lorenzo, joining in the lecture with fervor.

"Not personally, no." Dewey couldn't help herself.

"It's an amazing creature. It digs a trap—a cone in the sandy earth, into which unsuspecting ants, and other prey, tumble. Unable to escape—for the cone is constructed at such an angle that the poor creatures *cannot climb out*—the ant struggles and struggles anyway, much like Sisyphus with his rock. He may struggle for hours, perhaps an entire day. Upward lies salvation, but always the poor ant falls just short of the rim, until, exhausted, he tumbles backward into the waiting grasp of the predator. It's a very neat system. Very neat, indeed."

They were climbing as they walked, up a narrow defile on a dry hillside. The others in the group had disappeared over the crest of the hill, and Dewey felt her feet start to slip awkwardly in the dry, dusty trail. She thought of the prey in the ant lion's trap—this was how it must feel, surely, to struggle upward through the dust and the rocks, as though upward lay salvation. The hillside seemed to swim as Lorenzo's voice droned on, describing in minute detail the eventual death of the prey. When they finally reached the crest of the hill, she breathed a sigh of relief as she caught sight of George and the others, resting on a large flat rock under a shady tree.

"Hello there, you slowpokes," George said good-naturedly. He was seated beside Eloise, who looked as though she were a little bit sorry at Dewey's appearance. Dewey was momentarily taken aback; then she realized, with a start, that the widower George Farnham—reasonably handsome, moderately well-to-do, and extremely charming—might well be Eloise Morningside's cup of tea. As she made her way toward them, Dewey looked with new interest at Eloise Morningside. She noted the clear skin, the beautifully styled golden hair with just a touch of gray, the casual elegance of the clothes—straight out of a Ralph Lauren advertisement. Well, if you were the editor of *Faces* magazine you could afford to go to Elizabeth Arden all the time, to have your hair done by someone called Oscar or Rodolfo, to buy million-dollar clothes with that maddeningly perfect, perfectly casual air. Dewey looked scornfully down at her own well-worn dungarees, which sagged about the knees from long afternoons of weeding in the garden. It was time she retired them. Why had she waited so long? She looked back at Eloise and George and smiled her most brilliant smile. "I've been having a lesson in entomology."

"How *interesting*," commented Eloise. "Must be fascinating." She smiled, and Dewey noticed that Eloise was one of those women who always managed to have on the exact right amount of lipstick—not too much, not too little, and never smeary or goopy. Dewey herself was never able to pull that off. She had learned long ago not to expect miracles in the lipstick department.

George grinned at Dewey. "Did you learn a lot?"

"Oh, my heavens, yes. How could I help it?" Dewey was aware of Serena and Lorenzo hovering nearby.

"I can well imagine," Eloise put in acidly. "I hear their specialty is insects. And spiders. Ooh." She smiled at Dewey, a "just-we-girls" smile, which she then transferred to George—effecting, en route, a subtle transformation.

George smiled back. He was always so polite to everyone. That was one of his many fine characteristics.

Of course, to herself, Dewey pooh-poohed the notion that George might find Eloise interesting as well. George and Eloise Morningside! She, the infamous jet-setter and purveyor of gossip, panderer to all of the lowest reaches of the public's curiosity; he, the civic-minded, clear-thinking, small-town lawyer—independent, respectable, a lover of simple pleasures. The idea was preposterous.

Wasn't it?

"Dewey, are you listening?" George's voice held an irritated note.

"Sorry, George, I wasn't," Dewey admitted, as she took a seat on a tree stump near the group.

"I said that Eloise has been telling me about some of her more interesting lawsuits. You remember Randall Braxton, don't you?"

Dewey did indeed remember Randall Braxton—Randall Hazleton Braxton IV, to be precise, originally a fellow Hamiltonian. In spite of his numeric, Braxton came from a quiet farming family of very modest means. An ambitious political man, he had spurned his humble hometown, with its agrarian image, to take up residency and find a constituency in New York City, of all places. This prodigal son of Hamilton had been a member first of the state legislature and then of the House of Representatives, but too close an affiliation with big-time gamblers had brought about his downfall. Dewey now recalled how his enormous gambling debts—and the attendant intricacies of his dealings with crooked lobbyists and suspect politicians—had been exposed by *Faces*. Braxton's elderly parents had been mortified by the press coverage, which had been merciless, but nothing had been harder on them than the *Faces* exposé, which was particularly gloating with regard to the humbleness of his family background.

Dewey's face must have shown that the recollection brought her little pleasure. Randall the Fourth had no doubt been a trying, obnoxious man, but the episode of his public degradation had been painful for many Hamiltonians.

"I see your friend does recall him," Eloise said to George, her voice seeming suddenly more low-pitched and musical than ever. "We got rather a lot of mileage out of him, you know," she said, chuckling for George. She turned to Dewey. "Was he a close friend of yours?" Her eyes were wide with interest, sincere interest, no doubt.

"We knew each other," murmured Dewey, feeling slightly defensive. There was something about this Eloise that made her feel that way—defensive, and clumsy, and—well, old. There was no way around it. But Dewey knew that she and Eloise were probably the same age, or close to it. For some strange reason, this certainty made Dewey feel even older. "But of course in a little place like Hamilton, one does get to know one's neighbors rather well."

"I'm sure. Mr. Farnham here has been telling me what a delightful place it is." She patted George's knee ever so lightly. "You know, it's the kind of place I'd love to see someday." She looked straight at Dewey as she uttered this amazing phrase.

Dewey, to her great credit, was able to smile and answer swiftly. "You really should, you know. We have quite a nice hotel in town—old, rather elegant. Or, if you prefer, you're welcome to come and stay with me anytime you like. I have loads of rooms."

"Is that right?" Eloise Morningside smiled softly and looked at George as she uttered the question. "That's most kind of you, Mrs. James. Most kind."

"Call me Dewey."

"Very well. Dewey." Eloise's eyes shone. "And may I call you George?" She turned to George Farnham, whose face—it seemed to Dewey, anyway—brightened at the prospect.

"Of course," George replied.

"Well, now," Harriet Bray said heartily, breaking energetically into their little group. "You all are like turtles, sunning yourselves on this rock." She smiled at her seeming witticism. "Anyway, we'd better get a move on, as they say. It's about two miles back to the Hacienda, and there are some really great things to see between here and there. A stream runs down along the trail here, until it empties into a small laguna. There we'll see plenty of bird life, maybe even some eagles. Everyone ready?"

Everyone was ready. The Miltons, scowling, moved off as one; George ushered the two ladies ahead of him on the trail, leaving Harriet to listen to the wonders of nature photography.

Before long, Harriet began to point things out—plants, animals, and parts of the scenery in general. No doubt she knew her plants and animals, but poor Harriet was one of those condemned by nature to tell all she knew on every subject. Every tree, every shrub, every clump of dirt, it seemed, came within the scope of her casual and inexpert tutelage. Before the hike was ended, there would be little that the guests didn't know about the flora and fauna of the Escondida Valley.

Dewey was doing her very best to remain cheerful and interested. But in spite of herself, she sank deeper and deeper into a thoroughly terrible mood, restless and increasingly impatient with everyone around her. Ordinarily chipper enough to test the tolerance of more sobersided souls, she was suddenly out of sorts in the most surprising way, responding with marked brevity to the enthusiastic chatter of Harriet Bray, and the burblings and bubblings of the Lees. By the time they arrived back at the Hacienda, she was only fit company for the Miltons, which was a sad commentary indeed.

For the life of her, she couldn't fathom why.

9

IT DIDN'T TAKE long for the latest edition of the *Trumpeter* to reach Los Lobos. One of the staff—usually Mark Harris or Harriet Bray—went to Edmunds at least once a day to collect mail, pick up a few odds and ends, or often to meet or bid farewell to guests at Edmunds Field, the small private airport that the Hacienda owned and which saw about four takeoffs and landings each month. This morning Harriet had a severely sprained ankle, thanks to the sabotaging of her gym equipment. So it was Mark who drove the jeep down the winding road to town.

Mark Harris sensed that something was up from the moment he entered Patton's General Store. Fred Patton, a local merchant who had made a virtue out of ignoring his customers, rose from his corner stool as Mark entered, and beckoned to the young man. Mark, baffled, approached the counter.

"You tell your boss that we're all behind him on this," he said, indicating the *Trumpeter*.

Harris took one look at the front page and knew that they would all be in for trouble. He knew, too, that Sonia and Gerald were likely to want to shoot the messenger. He hurried back to Los Lobos, and by twelve-thirty Sonia and Gerald had decided on their strategy.

Shortly before lunch, the entire Los Lobos staff assembled awkwardly in the large kitchen. They had heard it all before, just last week, when the notes from "Monica" started to appear. The chef, Sidney Bachelor, and his associate Beverly leaned up against the counter; behind them was visible a small mountain of finely grated chocolate and large bowl of raspberries. In a corner near the door to the pantry, wearing chaps, heavy boots, and dirty denim shirts, were the three grooms, Carlitos, Chico, and Willy. Near them, three apple-cheeked, blue-uniformed maids were lined up in a row, like porcelain dolls on a shelf; and like dolls they seemed glassy-eyed and inert.

Harriet Bray had stationed herself close to the dining-room door, as far as possible from Charles Halifax, who was seated at the breakfast table, snacking on the corn bread that Sidney had baked for lunch. From her vantage point, Harriet could see that Charles's thighs had grown very fat; the flab on them hung down disgustingly over the edges of the rather narrow kitchen chair. She sniffed in satisfaction and unconsciously sucked in her trim stomach.

Gerald and Sonia stood near the sink, waiting patiently for the staff to quiet down. When the room was finally silent, Gerald began to speak.

"I don't think I need to tell you all why we have called this meeting. Do I." It was a statement, not a question. Nobody answered, and he went on. "This monkey business has got to stop. I am here to tell you that if things don't improve around here, I am prepared to fire each and every one of you, just to be certain we have rid ourselves of this plague of idiotic behavior. This is not a summer camp, this is the Hacienda Los Lobos."

There was a dull murmur as the threat was uttered. The maids turned their stare toward the floor. Charles Halifax yawned.

Gerald Clearwater turned to his wife. "Sonia?"

She nodded, and began to look around the room. She fixed each person in it with a brief glower. The maids,

compelled by her command, lifted their eyes as one. The
color had drained from their cheeks.

When her basilisk eye had made the circuit of the room,
Sonia held up the copy of that week's *Trumpeter* and spoke
in clear tones. "This is an absurdity. Is there anyone here
who does not find it so?"

The silence grew larger as Sonia waited for a response.

"Good," she said finally. "Now." She put the paper down
and drew a small spiral-bound notebook from her pocket.
"Each of you will describe to me the last visit you paid to
town. Who you saw, talked to, and what you did. You will
also tell me where you were yesterday morning between
nine and eleven. Let's start with you, Sidney."

She addressed the chef, who looked startled but instantly
obliged with an account of his movements. He had gone to
town last week, on Friday, to have his hair cut at Samson 'n'
Delilah, the unisex hair stylist in Edmunds. He had driven
on over to Villaseca later, to pick up a side of beef. As for
yesterday morning, both he and Beverly had been in the
kitchen; Beverly had been chopping vegetables for the
gazpacho and he had been making a list for the market.
Sonia took it all down, nodded, and went on to the grooms.
She addressed them in her fluent Spanish, and they answered her questions in turn.

It took half an hour to complete the record of everyone's
movements. When she was finished, Sonia nodded again.
"Thank you. I suggest everyone get back to work—but
before you do, I will tell you. If I ever see another flagrantly
hostile article in this rag"—she held up the *Trumpeter*—
"or if one word of yesterday morning's mishap goes beyond
the Hacienda, I will personally track down the person who
leaked the information, and that person will be dismissed on
the spot." She repeated the command in Spanish. "Understood?"

There were nods and much shuffling of feet.

"We have a reputation to maintain, and a loyal clientele to protect. Anyone on this staff who cannot put those goals first is welcome to leave right now."

There was no response.

"Fine," Sonia said briskly. "Now get back to work. We're late with the lunch." She and Gerald left.

There was a momentary prolongation of the silence behind their retreating backs, and then a heated argument broke out between one of the maids and Willy, the youngest of the three grooms.

10

DESPITE HAVING BEEN recently raked over the coals, Sidney Bachelor, the Los Lobos chef, was about to make one of George Farnham's fondest dreams come true. At nine on Wednesday morning George slipped into an apron, donned a white baseball cap, and waited impatiently in the Los Lobos kitchen for Sidney to make his appearance.

Widely admired in Hamilton for his gourmet table, George had long dreamed of cooking with a famous chef—and Sidney, at Los Lobos, was about as famous as they came. The table was one of the chief reasons that people came back, again and again, for a pricey stay at the ranch; Sidney had been cooking at Los Lobos for nearly thirty years, almost since the day that Sonia and Gerald had decided to turn the old family property into an inn.

The menu for the day's lunch was simple: grilled fresh brook trout with lemon-and-caper sauce, potatoes with butter and parsley, a salad of endive and radicchio, freshly baked bread, and a strawberry cobbler for dessert. Strawberry cobbler, as it happened, was one of George Farnham's great strengths; Sidney had agreed to let George make it. Not only that, but he also put George in charge of the potatoes and the salad dressing—an act of faith that George regarded as a genuine compliment. Salad dressings could be tricky, and tended to be more important with a simple meal like today's lunch. The trout, with its lemon-and-caper sauce, Sidney reserved for himself. His trout recipes were his long suit, and George deferred to the chef's experience.

Sidney's assistant, Beverly, was already in the kitchen, kneading the dough for today's bread. They exchanged a few polite words. Beverly was about twenty-five, with shining dark hair and sparkling blue eyes. She told George that she had come west to escape the confines of her New York City apartment and to salve a broken heart. So far, the fresh air and the slow pace of the Hacienda had agreed with her.

"Big change from New York, anyway," said Beverly, kneading.

"I can imagine. What were you doing there?"

"Cooking. I lived with a family—an older couple, really. They let me have the maid's room, and in exchange I made lunch and dinner for them every day."

"Sounds like a good setup."

"It was, for a while, but I did get a little tired of it. If you have to cook just for two people, and they happen to be sort of fussy, it can get a little stale."

"I suppose so." George watched Beverly pound the dough enthusiastically.

"Plus, this is a great opportunity for me. Sidney's famous, you know."

"I know," George replied. He picked up a small jar and sniffed at it. Powdered ginger.

"But he's not very practical," Beverly went on. "He's got this great reputation, but unfortunately he doesn't want to do anything but cook."

"Something wrong with that?" George had a twinkle in his eye. Beverly seemed like the kind of young woman who wouldn't miss the main chance. Undoubtedly she had thought up a clever scheme.

"Well, I had this idea," she replied. "You can tell me what

you think. We're going to start up a newsletter—a subscription thing. It will be really expensive, and come out just six times a year, and have about two menus in each issue. We'll tell all the people who come here that it's only offered to Los Lobos regulars, which will make them want it. The people who come here are like that."

"Hmm. Interesting idea. Yours?" George reached for a strawberry and popped it in his mouth.

"Yeah. I'm always thinking." Beverly grinned. "And luckily, with Sidney around, I've got something I can trade on. It takes more than brains to get rich."

"So it does," George agreed.

"I figure I'll do all the work, and Sidney can just put his name on it, and then it will be fair to split the profits."

"Fifty-fifty?"

"Well—not at first. More like eighty-twenty. But that will be negotiable in a year's time."

"That Beverly," said Sidney, finally making his appearance. "She's got a head on her shoulders, that girl." He winked at George. "Now, if I could only teach her to cook."

Beverly tossed a lump of dough at him; he caught it good-naturedly and threw it back at her. Then he turned to George, and the two of them got to work.

By eleven-thirty, nearly all was in readiness, except for the trout, which would be sautéed just at lunchtime. George's strawberry cobbler was a masterpiece, crisp and golden-brown on top. And his salad dressing was something else again; the locally produced honey, it seemed, added a very slight but unmistakable twist to the flavor. George dipped an endive leaf in the dressing, sampled it, nodded to himself, and thanked Sidney and Beverly. Then he took himself off to find Dewey, who was poking about the place, trying to find a clue to the identity of the "ghost."

*   *   *

Dewey, in her researches, had not turned up much. She had had another unsatisfying conversation with Charles Halifax, and she was on her way back to her room when she nearly collided with Eloise Morningside.

"Oh, I beg your pardon," said Dewey. "I'm afraid I sometimes just get wrapped up in my thoughts."

"Do you, now?" Eloise asked casually.

"Inclined to be abstracted, I'm afraid." She smiled at Eloise, who returned a remote echo of a grin. "Have you been playing tennis?" Now, that was a stupid question, Dewey, my girl, thought Dewey. In her tennis skirt, with racquet in hand, what else might Eloise have been doing?

"Oh, yes. I had a game with Mark Harris. He's the nicest young man."

"Yes, I thought so, too," remarked Dewey, who had had the chance to talk to him earlier that day. "Have you been riding yet?"

"Oh, no. I don't ride," replied Eloise. "Actually, don't tell anyone—but I'm scared to death of horses."

"Dear me! No, I won't tell a soul," Dewey promised. She bade Eloise good day and headed for her room.

Now, as she dressed for lunch, Dewey thought over that conversation. There was something not quite right in the encounter; or perhaps Eloise just made her feel old, and odd, and out of it. No, there had been something funny in Eloise's manner; and as she sat down on her bed to think things through, Dewey finally realized what it was. If she was not very much mistaken, Eloise had been coming out of the room next door to Dewey's. But that was George's room, not Eloise's.

The guests soon sat down outside on the terrace, under the hundred-year-old magnolia, for a beautiful lunch. The

Miltons, in matching scowls, arrived at the table, nodded morosely to their fellow guests, and took their seats in silence. Serena and Lorenzo bounded in a moment later, their Birkenstocks flapping, and chatted merrily about the trap-door spider's nest that they had found that morning. The creature was, they told the assembled group, an absolutely amazing example of the rather rare Western species known as the Thorn-loving Trap-door Spider, for its tendency to make its home at the foot of acacia trees. Using the sugar bowl, a raisin, and a small crust of bread, they illustrated the insect's technique of scurrying out of its hole to capture prey, then scurrying back in and closing the trapdoor behind it.

Sonia and Gerald listened politely; Dewey wondered briefly how they managed to appear so genuinely interested in their guests. But of course the guests were paying for the privilege of boring everyone silly, and for what Los Lobos charged, Sonia and Gerald could afford to be bored from time to time.

Eloise Morningside, looking crisp in linen trousers of olive-green, with a pale ivory silk blouse and an exotic-looking, African-print scarf about her neck, was the last to arrive. The others had gone ahead with their lunch, at her insistence. She had been sending off her monthly editorial, using the fax in Gerald's office.

"Terribly sorry not to be on hand for the great occasion," she breathed, pulling up a chair and neatly edging Dewey so that she could sit next to George. "They can't seem to manage without me," she complained, with a smile for everyone. "Here I am, a career woman, prepared to pay homage to you." She raised her wineglass to George.

"To me?" asked George, sounding surprised.

"Yes. I can do many things, but the one thing I can't do is cook. Can't bear it. I would never have the nerve to enter

Sidney's kitchen." She smiled and smoothed the crease on her safari trousers. "Like setting foot in a lion's den." She gave him a warm smile that seemed to congratulate him for his bravery. George took it all in stride.

George's strawberry cobbler was delicious, and everybody seemed to enjoy it thoroughly. "It's comforting to know, George," Eloise Morningside was saying, "that while I was practicing my serve this morning, you were looking after our creature comforts. This is absolutely *perfect*. Absolutely *heaven*. I adore a man who can cook. Don't you, Mrs. James, er, Dewey?"

"Absolutely," Dewey agreed firmly, without a trace of irony in her voice. George's skill in the kitchen was something that Dewey generally took for granted, but she did feel rather proud of him here today. "George is fabulously talented. We're all rather proud of him, back home in Hamilton."

"You must be," agreed Eloise, with a long look at George.

"She'd be better off trying to catch Sidney," Gerald whispered to Dewey, with a chuckle. Dewey merely smiled politely in return, putting on her best old-lady-at-sea air. She was in fact no longer paying the slightest attention to George and Eloise; it was Mark Harris who had caught her notice. He had appeared around the corner from the side entrance to the kitchen, with a look of utter desperation on his face. He quickly succeeded in getting Sonia's attention; she excused herself and followed him, an expression of mild annoyance on her face.

Three minutes later she reappeared, an urgent look in her eye, and summoned her husband.

Gerald gave her a startled look. Then he glanced apologetically around the table, and finally addressed the Miltons, who were frowning down at their untouched strawberry cobbler. Dewey supposed that Harriet Bray had been lecturing them on the evils of sweets—or perhaps they didn't need to be convinced. "Excuse me, won't you?" Gerald said politely. Philip Milton looked up, startled, and nodded. Gerald joined his wife, and they headed off together toward the south wing, where the staff had their rooms.

Dewey managed to get through her dessert without displaying any impatience. She listened as Lorenzo and Serena, in their antiphonal way, related still more horrible tales of predator and prey, but her mind was elsewhere, and she was vaguely conscious of a nervous dread. From the look on Sonia's face, Dewey guessed that perhaps the pranks at Los Lobos had finally gone too far. While Beverly served coffee, Dewey excused herself and headed for her room. Then she snuck out through a back door, and around through the kitchen yard toward the south wing, where the staff rooms were.

11

Despite the warm afternoon sunlight, a chill had descended at Los Lobos. Since lunch, Sonia and her staff had worked hard to dispel it; an excellent hostess by nature as well as by profession, Sonia managed to make sure that everyone was at his ease. More to the point, only Dewey and George knew that anything was really the matter; the arrival and departure of the paramedic team from Edmunds had taken place through the service entrance, while most of the guests were enjoying a cool siesta in their rooms. By the time the cocktail hour had arrived, all that remained was the waiting, and from this the guests were mercifully spared.

All except for Dewey and George, who were drinking sherry in the red parlor with Sonia. Gerald had gone down to Edmunds, to await results at the clinic.

"Tell me again what the staff think happened," Dewey demanded.

"They're saying that someone poisoned her."

"How?"

"At lunch. The staff ate in the kitchen, and apparently Harriet must have felt ill right away, and gone to her room. It was just the sheerest luck that Mark Harris went by when he did."

George studied his sherry glass earnestly, while Dewey protested. "But Harriet ate the same lunch that we all ate. It's impossible."

"The poison wasn't necessarily in the lunch," said Sonia soothingly, with a look at George.

To judge by the expression on George Farnham's face, he had determined not to take this event personally. Harriet Bray had been taken drastically ill in the middle of lunch, but there was no telling what had happened. George knew for a fact that he hadn't put any poison in the lunch, and the rest of them were perfectly fine. So he would just wait and see.

There was the sound of a car out in the main driveway, and a few moments later Gerald Clearwater entered. He had aged about twenty years; his face was gray, and his cheeks sagged. He headed straight for the antique drop-leaf table in the corner, which served as a bar. He nodded vaguely at Dewey and George as he passed them.

Sonia took a deep breath. "Is she all right, Gerald?" To everyone else in the room, the question seemed absurdly out of place. Quite clearly, Harriet Bray was not all right.

Gerald poured himself a stiff whiskey and drank it in one go. Then he turned to face his wife, and there was little need to ask what had happened.

"She died at five-thirty, more or less. There was nothing they could do, apparently."

There was a long silence in the room, which Sonia finally broke. "Died?" The disbelief in her voice was natural; the idea seemed absurd. Harriet Bray had died? "I don't quite see how that's possible, Gerald."

Gerald shook his head. "She suffered anaphylactic shock, as a result of a severe allergic reaction." He was quoting, obviously, the doctor's words.

"A reaction to what?" Sonia demanded.

Gerald shrugged. "They don't know. But the girl was allergic to all kinds of wacky things."

Dewey nodded. She well remembered how Harriet had

told anyone who would listen about her allergies to all sorts of foods. Well, that was an end to it. The young woman's death, especially in the prevailing atmosphere of persecution at Los Lobos, was a terribly unfortunate event. Thank heaven it was nothing more than that.

Dewey glanced toward George, who smiled gamely. "Shall we dress for dinner, my dear?"

"Excellent suggestion," Dewey agreed.

"Wait a minute," insisted Sonia. "Not so fast." She gave Dewey a pained look. "I mean, Dewey, you must see—" She looked at her husband. "They've been talking all afternoon about how that girl was poisoned."

"Poisoned!" Gerald was shocked. "That's ridiculous."

"They're saying it's Monica's ghost again," Sonia went on. "You know how superstitious some of those people can be, Gerald. All we need is for Larry Ceboll to write another one of his famous 'news' articles, and we're done for."

Gerald, who hadn't moved from the bar, poured himself another whiskey. "Why on earth would anyone poison that girl?" he asked, his back to them.

Sonia looked at Dewey, who looked thoughtful. "Do you know of any reason?" Dewey asked. "Be honest. Is there anything, something about that girl that might have made her a target?"

"No. Absolutely nothing. Well, Dewey, you met her. All she wanted out of life was a gymnasium and people to take her aerobics classes. A very uncomplicated girl, open as a book, with small ambitions that were perfectly within reason."

"Then you have absolutely nothing to fear." She rose, ready to leave. The Clearwaters would need to think about how to break the news to the rest of the staff, as well as to the guests.

"I see that this will be a very difficult time for you,

Sonia," Dewey said. "But if anyone is talking about poisons, you simply confront them with the doctor's report. The woman died from an allergic reaction—an extremely tragic event, but purely an accident. It could have happened anywhere or anytime."

"I suppose you're right about that," Sonia agreed, sounding despondent.

"Just keep it in mind. Don't let anybody persuade you otherwise." She and George left and headed across the main courtyard toward their rooms in the west wing.

12

IT DIDN'T TAKE long for news of Harriet Bray's death to make the rounds. The guests at the Hacienda were told of it right away, as they assembled for cocktails on the large front porch, just before dinner that evening.

Gerald cleared his throat and knocked a spoon against his glass for attention. Everyone looked up curiously, and he fixed on Dewey as he addressed the small crowd.

"I am sorry to have to tell you this," he said, "but we have had an unfortunate accident here today." There was a deep silence while everyone gave him their attention. He leaned back against the porch railing; behind him, the sun was going down over the orchard. Dewey thought Gerald looked more rumpled and disoriented than ever; his necktie was poorly tied, and his jacket looked as though it had just come out from under someone's mattress. No doubt, the news of the young woman's death had hit him hard.

"I am sorry to tell you that our aerobics instructor, Harriet Bray, was taken ill earlier in the day. Apparently she suffered a severe allergic reaction to something that she ate at lunchtime."

"Is she all right?" interposed Serena, her voice commanding Gerald's full attention.

"Er, no." Gerald cleared his throat. "No. I'm afraid not. According to the doctors at the hospital here in Edmunds, she suffered acute anaphylactic shock. I am terribly sorry to tell you that she died a few hours ago."

There was a momentary silence as the guests digested this information. Belinda Milton was the first to speak. "Died?" Her voice was incredulous. "That young woman *died* this afternoon?"

"I'm afraid so," said Gerald, looking miserably uncomfortable. "Sonia and I thought it best that we should tell you all, right now, in this way. The last thing we want is for any of our guests to be upset or worried by this terribly unfortunate event."

"I don't understand. How could she have died?" Philip Milton sounded as though he'd get to the bottom of it, as though there must be some misconception.

Gerald cleared his throat and held a hand out to them, palm forward, asking their indulgence. "Harriet was allergic to all kinds of things, and unfortunately her allergic reaction was extremely severe. She was accustomed to living at risk of such a reaction. It is just terribly tragic that no one here was able to do anything to save her."

There was an awkward silence as Gerald finished his little speech, but the chatter returned to normal embarrassingly quickly. Charles Halifax said, in a voice loud enough for everyone to hear, that he wouldn't pretend to a grief he could not feel; Mark Harris was noncommittal but quiet. Eloise Morningside didn't appear to be quite sure who Harriet Bray was, but she agreed the death was tragic. Then she poured herself a second margarita from the pitcher on the table.

Serena and Lorenzo shook their heads. In their overlapping way, they eulogized poor Harriet, agreeing with each other that her death might have been gratifying to her, had she known what kind of death it was, because it was so natural. They themselves found it a great comfort that Harriet's going was a part of Nature. Oddly, the Miltons seemed most upset. Dewey found this rather surprising; she was glad to see that they had, after all, a streak of humanity about them. Perhaps they were just people who could only rise to gloomy occasions. Certainly they had begun to show more animation in the last fifteen minutes than they had shown in the previous two days.

"I really enjoyed that nature walk she took us on yesterday," Belinda Milton said to Dewey, who was willing to listen. "I enjoyed it. So did Philip."

Philip Milton nodded to show the accuracy of his wife's allegation. "Better than anything else this dump has to offer," he said offensively.

"Don't you like it here?" asked Dewey, genuinely surprised. Why would anybody bother to stay at Los Lobos if they didn't like it?

"No. It's boring, and our bedspread has all kinds of holes in it, and our shower comes out in a trickle. Some nerve these people have, charging all this money and not even giving you a decent shower."

"Mmm," said Dewey. She didn't mind the low water pressure—nor the bedspreads with holes, which were two-hundred-year-old Spanish lace, and probably worth a fortune. "Then—"

Belinda Milton cut her off. "My brother-in-law was the one who got us into this in the first place. He and Philip's sister come here all the time." She glared at her husband. It was all his fault, obviously.

"Well, I think it's rather nice, myself," Dewey said politely. "But then, where I come from we don't have much in the way of Spanish influence. So Los Lobos is very exotic."

"I could live without the Spanish influence, myself," Philip Milton responded tartly. "You get a little sick of it when you have to live with it."

"That's for sure," Belinda Milton put in.

Dewey wondered where on earth the Miltons might be happy. In a sealed, hygenic plastic cube, maybe. Or perhaps underground, with those strange, strange people who had gone to live in a hermetically sealed underground utopia. She was spared having to respond by the sound of the dinner gong. Saved by the bell, she thought, excusing herself and darting toward the dining room.

The mood around the enormous table was subdued, and the feeling was heightened by the candlelight and the heavy antique furniture, and the scowling brow of Felipe Torcaza, Gerald's great-great grandfather, who frowned disapprovingly from a portrait on the north wall. Sonia and Gerald exerted themselves to find charming topics of dinner-table conversation; as the waiter passed with a serving dish of creamed spinach, Dewey reflected that it must be difficult under the best of circumstances to keep the conversation lively. Tonight it would be a real challenge.

Sonia and Gerald, however, rose to the challenge. Gerald produced, as a topic of conversation, his great-uncle Horacio, who allegedly had been a sort of desert bandit of the nineteenth century. He had swooped down upon unsuspecting cross-continent voyagers and stolen from them extensively—food supplies, fabric, tools, and arms that they had so painstakingly carried with them in their journey westward. The stolen goods were offered for sale in the general store, at a deeply discounted price. "He saved a great deal on freight," Sonia explained, with a twinkle in her eye.

"Not to mention cost of goods sold," added George Farnham.

"An accountant's dream," Gerald agreed. Great-uncle Horacio, however, had been blessed with a sense of justice; he always made sure the travelers had enough supplies left to arrive safely at their destination. He also provided them with a crude map detailing the rest of their journey, pointing out places where they might encounter hostile tribes and telling them how and where to pan for gold. Great-uncle Horacio's tips were usually accurate; his victims arrived safely, and they grew wealthy on his insider's information. Generally speaking, there were no hard feelings.

"I find it hard to believe," Eloise Morningside insisted, "that Great-uncle Horacio would just give away that sort of information."

"Ah, but you can see he was cutting into the competition when he did so. He was an amazingly shrewd business-man." Gerald Clearwater sighed. If he were half as shrewd, he wouldn't need to be so worried about the future of Los Lobos.

Sonia agreed. "He only cared about his own territory, a small swath of the stage and wagon route between here and St. Louis. There's an awful lot of other ground that has to be covered."

"Very practical," murmured Dewey, not at all sure that she liked Great-uncle Horacio. "Did he have many friends?"

"Not a one," admitted Gerald. "He was a true *lobo*—a real wolf. He's not someone to emulate, but his money helped to keep the family farm together for quite a while. I don't look up to him, but I am grateful to him. And he was careful not to hurt people."

"He was," Sonia agreed loyally. "Besides, the trip here from St. Louis was so dreadfully dangerous that I think maybe, in a way, people were glad to encounter Horacio. The rest of the trip was so full of scorpions and rattlesnakes, and people were constantly losing their way, or dying from some mysterious disease. A bandit was at least a known quantity."

There was an appreciative silence, as the diners considered Great-uncle Horacio. It was difficult not to envy the man's sangfroid, but the fascination with the bandit uncle melted away as everyone's thoughts returned to the startling death of Harriet Bray. Typically, Serena and Lorenzo were the first to speak.

"Nature is still full of hidden dangers for us, isn't that right, Lorenzo?" Lorenzo nodded his agreement as Serena looked mildly around the table. "That poor girl who died today."

The other guests squirmed in their chairs, but Lorenzo took up the torch. "Yes, she was simply confronting the natural challenges of life. It is the job of the scientist and the lover of Nature to elucidate such dangers, but we can't eliminate them, can we, my sweet?"

"No," Serena said, a touch mournfully. "We can't eliminate them."

Dewey, seeing that Sonia and Gerald were monstrously uncomfortable, leapt in. "On the other hand," she said, "Great-uncle Horacio must have had tremendous knowledge of the territory. He was a scholar, in his own way, wasn't he?"

Sonia threw Dewey a grateful look, and the conversation became lively once more. Poor Harriet Bray was nearly forgotten as the Clearwaters and their guests discussed the exploration of the American West. In the library, Gerald had some maps, diaries, and drawings left over from Great-uncle Horacio's estate, which provided distraction enough for nearly everyone in the group. This was lucky, because everything would be different tomorrow.

Larry Ceboll was busy typing up his lead story when the phone rang. It was Packy Tate.

"Yeah?" said Ceboll, taking a huge bite of a liverwurst sandwich.

"Mr. Ceboll, it's me, Sheriff Tate."

"Packy, you old hound." Ceboll took a huge swallow of beer, belched loudly, and wiped his mouth. "What's up?"

"Well, I thought maybe we should meet."

"Meet?" A strange thing for the sheriff to say. All he had to do was come by.

"Um, yeah. Mr. Ceboll, I think I'm finding out something that would interest you. If you know what I mean."

Ceboll belched again and squinted through the dusty window to the street outside. Six o'clock in the afternoon; the only things stirring in Edmunds were the flies. Packy Tate, because he worked for the county, had his office outside of town, halfway between here and Villaseca. Ceboll wasn't really doing anything important; he almost never did anything important. He could be at the sheriff's office in fifteen.

But it wouldn't do to be too eager. He knew exactly what Packy Tate was after—he wanted to see that note torn up, or burned, once and for all.

It might just be worth it. Tate almost never picked up the phone to call in with anything. Just came by as usual with his weekly log of crimes. His call meant that there was something brewing up at Los Lobos.

"Just come on by, Mr. Ceboll. I can't leave right now. I'm on duty, and the deputy's in Villaseca, collecting the money from the parking meters."

"All right," said Ceboll. "I was going to Villaseca anyway to get a few things." He glanced at his watch. "I'll be there in a while."

He chowed down the rest of the liverwurst and hopped into his pickup. This was going to be good. He could just smell it.

13

MATTHEW LITTLE, THE Lincoln County medical examiner, was a bulky six-footer with blue eyes and a deceivingly casual air about him. He served not only as the county medical examiner, but also as a general practitioner in both Edmunds and Villaseca; he was a well-rounded physician of the old-fashioned sort, who still made house calls and had both pediatric and geriatric patients, along with everything in between. After thirty-seven years of practice in the two small towns, he could boast that he knew just about everyone there was to know, inside and out.

He and the Clearwaters had a long acquaintance that bordered, in the way of such things, on friendship. Gerald was surprised, but not alarmed, when Little turned up to see him at eight o'clock on Thursday morning. Little told Gerald that they needed to speak privately, and the two men headed discreetly for the office.

"Yesterday I examined that instructor of yours, Gerry," said Little, sipping at a cup of fresh-brewed coffee. Hospitality never failed at Los Lobos.

"I thought that must be it." Gerald Clearwater regarded Little carefully. "And?"

"It appears that she ingested a very large quantity of mustard, which caused a severe allergic reaction."

"Mustard." Gerald Clearwater appeared to be thinking this news through. "And that's what killed her?"

"I believe so. According to Dr. Ward, who saw her at the

clinic, you told the paramedics that she suffered from allergies."

"That's right. She was allergic to just about everything, that girl. You name it, it gave her hives or heebie-jeebies or something." Gerald thought about it. "We had no way of knowing how much of it was true, of course, and it seemed excessive to me, but then I've never been the allergic type."

"Well, she must not have realized that her sensitivity extended to mustard." Little finished his coffee and gave Gerald an encouraging look. "You don't need to feel like any of this was your fault. There isn't anything anyone could have done to prevent it, you know."

"No, no." Clearwater took a distracted sip of coffee. "Well, then, Little." He rose. "I thank you for coming by. Anything I need to do?"

"Well, I suppose in order to sign the death certificate I should probably just have a word with Sidney. All right with you?"

Clearwater managed a casual grin, but there was a wariness about his pale blue eyes. "Absolutely." His voice was hearty. "Let's go find him." They left the office and headed for the kitchen wing. Clearwater kept his demeanor cheerful; there was no point in thinking the worst until you knew that you had no choice. But Sonia took one look at her husband, as he and Little passed through the dining room, and she knew that something was wrong.

The three of them went through the swinging door and found Sidney stirring stock. He gave Clearwater a distracted nod. "Morning, Gerald," he said, barely turning around. Out of the corner of his eye, he saw Matthew Little. Sidney dropped his wooden spoon and came forward to greet the medical examiner.

"Little," he said, shaking hands.

"Morning, Sidney. I think you probably know why I'm here."

"About that young woman."

Little nodded. "I just wanted to confirm the findings from the autopsy." Sidney looked grim, and Little waded on. "It seems likely that the reaction was caused by something ingested at lunch. She was eating lunch, wasn't she, when she first became ill?"

"I think so, but I really can't be sure."

Gerald Clearwater interrupted. "But wasn't everyone right here? All the staff were having their lunch, weren't they, Sidney?" He gestured to the long table in the far corner where the staff generally ate. "That's what I understood."

Sidney looked momentarily perplexed. "She was having lunch, I think. But not here. In her room."

"In her room? Why?" asked Gerald.

Matthew Little held up a hand to interrupt. They were getting off the subject. "The location isn't important, Sid," Little said. "But what she ate is important. What did she eat that had mustard in it?"

"Mustard?" Now Sidney was genuinely puzzled. "Nothing. No—we were always really careful about that with Harriet. If there was mustard in something, I told her about it. But I didn't need to worry about remembering. She always asked. Always." Sidney kept his voice polite, but even so it was evident that Harriet's constant questions had sometimes been burdensome.

"Did she ask you yesterday?" asked Sonia, joining the conversation for the first time. The men looked around in surprise. Nobody had realized that she was there in the kitchen with them.

"Yup. She asked, and I answered. No, there wasn't any mustard. Not on the trout, of course, and not on the potatoes, and not in the salad, and not in the bread, and not in the dessert."

"You're sure of that?" Little sounded uneasy.

"Positive."

Little was silent for a moment, allowing the implication to sink in. Either Sidney was mistaken, or the lab report was wrong. It was evident which way Little was leaning.

"Sidney, what about the salad dressing? That's a place where people use mustard a lot."

Gerald cleared his throat and looked inquisitively at his wife, who nodded.

"I know what you're thinking, Sonia," replied Sidney, in a voice filled with assurance. "Don't forget I also ate the lunch. Plus, I was watching the whole time. No mustard."

"Watching what or whom?" asked Matthew Little, his tone sharp.

"It's not important," Sonia put in hastily.

"Let me decide what's important, Sonia." Little was all authority now. He returned his gaze to Sidney. "What were you watching?"

"I had some help with the lunch yesterday. But it's immaterial. There was no mustard."

"You mean you didn't make the salad dressing." There was silence. "Okay, Sidney. I know she's a cute little New Yorker, but I think I'd better have a word with her." He looked at Sonia, who didn't budge. "Sonia?"

Sidney held up a hand. "Beverly didn't make the dressing. She was busy with the béchamel for dinner."

"Great. Who made it, Sidney?" Little was running out of patience.

Sonia nodded discreetly, and Sidney finally answered. "One of the guests."

"Oh, boy." Little's face fell. He suddenly understood why everyone was acting so strange. This was certainly an unlooked for complication, but it could also be the answer. "All right. Tell me who."

"Never mind that, Little," Sonia insisted stubbornly. "Let me worry about that."

"Afraid I can't, Sonia. This is a legal matter as well as a medical one."

"Yes, but you can at least let me approach my guest first with some innocent questions."

Matthew Little sighed and gave in.

"Sidney—" Sonia began. Little held up a hand, and kept his gaze fixed on Sidney.

The chef took a moment to think it through. "I think we can settle this once and for all," he said at last. "We have some dressing left over. I was going to use it as a base for tonight's marinade." He strode to the refrigerator—a huge old thing with a massive stainless steel door. He reached inside and brought out a small ceramic bowl, covered with plastic and half full of salad dressing. Then he produced a leaf of lettuce. He handed the two to Matthew Little. "This is the leftover dressing. See for yourself."

Sidney stepped back, crossed his arms, and waited. Matthew Little was a big man, but Sidney had him by four or five inches. He looked down his nose at the coroner, who lifted the plastic wrap, dipped the leaf in, and sampled.

Little's eyebrows shot up, and he coughed loudly. Then he handed the jar to Sidney. "You got a cold or something, bub?"

Sidney frowned and reached in the refrigerator for another lettuce leaf. He tore it into thirds and offered segments to Sonia and Gerald; the three of them dipped the lettuce ceremoniously and, as one, tasted.

"I think maybe you misremembered," suggested Little, watching their expressions.

Sidney looked ready to protest, but opted out. He shrugged

his shoulders and glared at Sonia, as if to say, "Get this cretin out of my kitchen."

Sonia and Gerald hustled Little out into the passageway. The coroner looked at them.

"Who made the dressing, Sonia?"

"I'm not telling you."

"Oh, for Pete's sake—"

"Not just yet, anyway." She gave Little a stern look. "Matthew, this situation is just full of problems. Such as, does Los Lobos face the possibility of a billion-dollar lawsuit from Harriet Bray's family? Is the guest liable? Are we facing manslaughter charges here? Will our catering license be revoked?"

Matthew Little nodded. He began to see the scope of the problem. He told Sonia and Gerald that he would give them twenty-four hours to inform him properly regarding the authorship of the salad dressing.

He left shortly, and Sonia and Gerald looked at each other in dismay. There was no question about it; George's dressing was loaded with mustard.

14

"NONE. ABSOLUTELY NOT," said George Farnham. "There's no question about it." He was seated on the red velvet sofa in the parlor; in the heat of the mid-morning sun, the velvet seemed atrociously hot and inappropriate. Dewey, sitting next to him, was conscious of the weight of the fabric, and with her right hand she could feel a spot where the nap had worn thin. The fabric was cooler there.

She looked carefully at George, and knew that he spoke with absolute certainty. George Farnham was never mistaken in his recipes. "Sonia, I know George wouldn't make an error about something like that."

Sonia looked sharply at her old friend. "Dewey, what else are we to think?"

"Sonia's right," added Gerald. He was standing by the window, staring out over the front lawn, a glass of sherry in his hand. The visit of Matthew Little had visibly shaken him. "*You* might be certain, George, but how can we be sure?"

"You just have to take his word for it," Dewey retorted stoutly. "Surely, Gerald, you don't think that George could be mistaken about something so important?"

"Frankly, I don't know what to think," Gerald said sourly.

Dewey thought she understood. Probably Gerald had never much liked Harriet Bray—not that he considered likability an important qualification for employment, but the girl had gotten on his nerves. On everyone's nerves, if she were any judge. Charles Halifax, however, had been the only one who had been lax enough to let the annoyance show.

There had just been something irritating about Harriet—Dewey had felt it, too. She gave off an air of eagerness that bordered on desperation, as though you were her last chance at friendship, and your friendship would be the one thing that could help her out of whatever mess she was in. She was someone that you wanted to stay far away from—because if she got too close, you would inevitably hurt her feelings if you shook free of her. Dewey imagined that Harriet, as a young girl, had suffered mightily at the hands of other young girls. She would have been the sort of girl that the others bullied. She had seemed to ask for it.

"Remember why I'm here in the first place, Sonia. Los Lobos has been suffering a plague of thoughtless and idiotic pranks. Have you considered the possibility?"

Sonia looked surprised and interested by the idea. "I'll bet you're right, Dewey." She snapped her fingers. "It's just exactly the kind of thing our ghost would dream up." Her expression grew somber. "God, how perfectly ghastly. And I imagine there is one person here at Los Lobos who is feeling deeply ashamed."

"You think so?" asked Dewey. "If so, I haven't noticed it. No, I think your ghost isn't really as sensitive as all that."

By Thursday morning, Packy Tate was one happy sheriff. Mr. Ceboll had called him with the news: he had personally destroyed the promissory note, torn it right up and put it in the trash. That was Larry Ceboll's way of showing his gratitude.

Packy would have liked to have burned the thing himself, just to see it go up in smoke, and be sure it was gone for good. But you can't have everything, he realized. He figured, as he'd told Mr. Ceboll, that over time he'd given at least eight thousand bucks' worth of free services and information to the *Trumpeter* and its owner. But this latest thing had topped them all.

And it wasn't as though he had done anything wrong, really. By this morning, the town hall would have a public record of that girl's death, sent over by the Clinica Consuelo. But Packy Tate had made sure Ceboll got hold of the medical examiner's report, which wasn't supposed to be public, unless there was some reason for it. And he had promised to see Judge Baker, who owed him a favor, about an inquest. Judge Baker wasn't the coroner—that was Judge Hafter—but Judge Baker might be able to swing something. Mr. Ceboll had told him that the first step of their plan would be to have the judge take away the Los Lobos catering license, which was issued by Lincoln County. Up to now, there hadn't been any real reason that anybody could think of to do that. But now they had a reason. That girl had been as good as poisoned.

Before long, Mr. Ceboll would be sitting pretty up at Los Lobos. And Packy Tate would have put him there. Sheriff Tate knew how valuable such help could be.

Dewey and George were once more on horseback; they had agreed, without needing to discuss it, that the only place where they would be free to talk would be far from the house and well out in the open. Dewey had persuaded Carlitos to let them take the horses on their own, without a guide. The old man had clearly been impressed by Dewey's riding the other day, because he agreed readily.

George was growing rather fond of his chestnut mount, a honey of a horse called Hackey. Dewey was riding Mal Genio again; the name said it all. They had set off shortly after the discussion with Sonia and Gerald, following a trail that Carlitos had recommended as easy and relatively flat. George had had enough, on Tuesday, of narrow trails along precipitous cliff sides. Despite Hackey's evident sweetness and expertise, it was impossible for George to enjoy the view when he had his eyes closed.

Before long, they reached a sort of pasture area, where a large pine was growing and where several sheep, looking absentminded and timid, were grazing. From here you could see for several hundred yards in every direction; Dewey very much wanted to avoid being surprised by finding Charles Halifax, or anyone else, suddenly within earshot. She pulled her horse up, dismounted, and tied the reins to a convenient branch. George followed suit, and they took seats on the ground under the pine. The countryside was fine, but Dewey could tell that George was feeling very low. She needed him to be his cheerful self.

"It's terribly distressing, George, but it clearly has nothing to do with you."

"I know that," said George, "but I resent being the vehicle, however unwitting, of that girl's death."

"If you were."

"What do you mean, if I was?" He picked up a fallen pinecone and threw it at a nearby ewe, who bleated complacently and scampered awkwardly away. "Did you try that dressing? I did. It wasn't mine. It was an abomination."

"George, look at it rationally. Harriet Bray was always on the lookout for mustard. She drove the cook—"

"Chef," George corrected automatically.

"Yes, well then, Chef. She drove him batty with her constant questions about ingredients."

"That's true." George was beginning to come out of his sulk. "But I'm not sure what that means, my dear."

"Not only that," Dewey went on, "but I am quite sure

there wasn't a soul at this place who was unaware of Harriet's many allergic tendencies."

"Still, one doesn't always remember those things. I am quite sure I did *not* use mustard—not with endive, I wouldn't do that. On the other hand, there is no guarantee that I would remember to omit the mustard. No guarantee that an outsider would credit. I have only my culinary conscience."

"Which is, after all, rather strong." Dewey went back to her main point. "But on the other hand Harriet never let anyone forget, and she most certainly wouldn't forget to ask."

"No, maybe not." He frowned. "I still don't see where this gets us, Dewey."

"George." Dewey was beginning to think that her friend's brain had clouded over. She looked him firmly in the eye. "What is the most salient quality of mustard?"

"It's pungency," George replied automatically.

"Well, then. Please explain to me how on earth anyone as allergy-obsessed as Harriet Bray managed to swallow a lethal dose of mustard without noticing it?"

George's eyes lit up. "By gum, my dear, I believe you've raised an interesting point."

"Unless, of course, there were some effective way of concealing the flavor."

"With that lunch? I doubt it." George sounded self-assured again. He enumerated the ingredients. "Bread, butter, fresh brook trout with lemon-and-caper sauce, potatoes with parsley, and the salad—endive, radicchio, and a very mild faux mayonnaise dressing." He shook his head. "The flavor of mustard, of a lot of mustard, simply could not be concealed in that meal. Impossible." George stood up and reached a hand down to Dewey. "I feel much better, my dear." He helped her up.

Dewey, however, looked as though the wind had been taken out of her sails.

"What's wrong?"

"Well, George, what's wrong is this." She frowned in thought. "You see, if the medical examiner is correct about the mustard—I mean, if Harriet ate mustard—then how on earth did she not notice it?"

"But he must be wrong, don't you see?"

"No. I'm afraid that's what I do not see. I don't see how he could be mistaken."

"Now, look, Dewey—" George was upset. "We've just reached that conclusion. There's no way I could be mistaken. And even if I were, there's no way that Harriet Bray would have failed to notice it. We're off the hook."

"Yes—yes, so we are. But if we're off the hook, George, I'm very much afraid that someone else is on."

"Hmm? I don't follow you."

Dewey fixed him with a piercing look. "Don't you see it, George?" She shook her head sadly. "That poor girl."

"Now, Dewey—" George looked alarmed. He often felt that Dewey was inclined to let her imagination run ahead of her. "You're not going to say she was murdered?"

"Oh, indeed I am, George." Dewey's eyes had a faraway look. "Indeed. She was murdered." She fixed her friend with a vigorous stare. "What do you say we find out why, and by whom?"

15

"IF YOU PLEASE," Dewey said primly, "I need to see Dr. Little."

The heavyset woman behind the counter was about fifty-five, with bright red lips and a bright red dress; her tall hair had been dyed to match, but the effort was not a success. The plaque on the counter proclaimed her to be Nyna-Joan Rebacker, Reception.

"Yeah?"

"That is, Miss Rebacker, if he's free. My name is Dewey James."

"Hold on," said Nyna-Joan, and she hefted herself, grunting, from her chair and went off around the corner.

Dewey studied the place. The Lincoln County Medical Examiner's office made her uneasy, but she wasn't sure if her unease arose from her task or from the deplorable surroundings. The whitewashed cement walls looked as though they'd been designed for a prison; the only decorative accent was an aged, filthy, and torn tourist poster on the far wall, showing a sunset in the Escondida Valley in garish greens and blues and pinks. There was a rank of vinyl bowl chairs in bright blue and orange; they were attached by a long pole that ran underneath their seats, as though they might sneak off individually otherwise. It kept the visitors neatly in their place that way.

Dewey would simply state her case and leave. She and George had discussed it; it was clearly her duty to come. But this was not Hamilton, and she didn't have to remind herself that the local law-enforcement authorities might not take kindly to the opinions of a stranger. They might even consider Dewey to be intruding herself where she didn't belong, although heaven knew that was far, far from the case. She took a deep breath and steeled herself, ready to do what she considered right. The rest would follow.

Nyna-Joan Rebacker reappeared. "He'll be with you in a minute."

"Thank you." Dewey smiled primly. "This is a nice little town you've got here."

"You up at the ranch?"

"Yes, yes I am. And I must say it's a truly beautiful place. Have you seen it?"

"Sure. There's a local girl that used to work up there. Monica Toro."

"Oh. Monica is from Edmunds?"

"From Villaseca, next town over. Was. Was from Villaseca. She's the one what drownded last month."

"Oh, my heavens, how terrible."

"Yeah. It was pretty horrible. She was a nice girl. Smart, too. Well, she had to be smart. She used to be Larry Ceboll's secretary, and she lasted in that job a good six months, which is six times longer than the record. Plus she did it without letting him put a hand on her. So you just know she had to be smart."

"I see," said Dewey. She gathered the obvious about Larry Ceboll, and was on the point of pursuing the question further when Nyna-Joan's telephone rang. She answered it, said "Yeah," and hung up.

"Come on," she said, and Dewey followed meekly.

Dewey recognized Matthew Little—his visit to the Hacienda had not been lost on her. She wished him a polite good morning, explained who she was, and told him that she had something of importance to communicate.

"Important how?" asked Little. He gestured her to a seat—another vinyl bowl chair, but this one on its own, an escapee from the chain gang. Dewey was pleased by the prompt and cordial reception; the man seemed willing enough to listen. Perhaps he had ideas of his own about the case. Or perhaps he just didn't have anything else to do. There probably wasn't much business for the county medical examiner of Edmunds and Villaseca, Dewey reasoned; he might easily have time to spare.

"I've come about that girl, Harriet Bray. The one who died."

"Yes, I know her name."

"The thing is, you see, I have heard that she died from the complications of a severe allergic reaction to mustard."

"That's right." Little looked sternly at Dewey. "And since you're only a guest up there, Mrs. James, and presumably you haven't got a vested interest in the hotel business, maybe you'll tell me what went on, and why they're being so stubborn."

Aha! thought Dewey. This was why he was being so polite. He wanted something. "Stubborn? How?"

"The Clearwaters have refused to tell me the name of the person responsible."

"Well," said Dewey, looking shrewdly at the doctor, "there is a very good reason for that. That is because, so far, no one knows who is responsible."

"That's a lie." Little was impatient. "They know. That Sidney won't say, and he was right there the whole time. Probably has a guilty conscience, but he shouldn't let amateurs into his kitchen. I'm afraid this may ruin his reputation."

"No, I wouldn't say that," Dewey replied patiently. Little

was clearly furious with the Clearwaters and with everyone connected with Los Lobos. She would wait it out.

"And Sonia and Gerald ought to know better. They're trying to protect themselves, and they can't see what harm they're actually doing." He sighed heavily. "So that's why I leapt at the chance to talk to you, Mrs. James. Frankly, I am going to ask for your help."

"I will help you, I hope," said Dewey, feeling it was time to take control, "but first, let me tell you some of the things I have been thinking about. Because I have been doing quite a lot of thinking about all of this."

She described the path her thoughts had taken during her conversation with George that morning. "If you work from the assumption that there was no mustard in that dressing when it was prepared, then you have to come to the obvious conclusion."

Little had listened carefully. He was interested. The whole thing was weird from start to finish, but it made more sense her way than his way.

"I won't say it's obvious, but I'll go along for the sake of the argument."

"You are convinced that there was a lethal dose of mustard in the dressing," said Dewey. "But likewise we are convinced that no one in the kitchen—and I mean *no* one—put that mustard in."

"One problem, Mrs. James," Little said politely. "I tried it. Did you taste it?"

"No." Dewey shook her head. "But Sonia and Gerald told me all about it. That this morning, there was mustard. Where yesterday there had been none." She gave him a challenging look.

"But that's ridiculous."

"Not if you consider, Doctor, that we are dealing with a murderer who is trying to cover his tracks."

"A murderer?" Little tilted his head back and smiled. His eyes twinkled gently. "Now, what makes you say that?"

"There is no other logical explanation that will answer all the facts." Dewey was firm.

"Sure there is. It was a tragic accident. Now all we need is for the person who made the mistake to own up to it. Then we'll all feel better." He leaned forward and rested his arms on his desk, studying Dewey intently. "Was it you, Mrs. James? Is that why you came to see me?"

"Absolutely not," said Dewey, firmly but politely. "If you knew me better, Dr. Little, you wouldn't ask. My friends know that the only thing I'm capable of in the kitchen is boiling an egg."

"A sophisticated person like yourself?" Little was clearly disappointed, but he was polite.

"I assure you, Doctor, that is the case. I'm probably capable of poisoning someone, but not of making salad dressing that everyone else at Los Lobos would eat." She shrugged her shoulders. "I wish I knew how to persuade you."

"That the girl was murdered?"

"Yes. Because, you see, there really isn't any other answer to the problem. Not if you grant that the rest of us are speaking the truth. And it is far more reasonable for us to speak the truth than otherwise. If we are speaking the truth, then there was some reason to put mustard in the dressing *after* it had been served to everyone."

"As ridiculous as that seems."

"It only seems ridiculous if you make the mistake of thinking that the girl died accidentally. Which is just what the murderer wants you to think." Dewey paused for breath. She had encountered this kind of skepticism before. "I know what you're thinking," she said.

"You do?"

"Yes. You're wondering what on earth got into the old lady's head to make her dream up such things."

"Well, I—"

"That's quite all right, you don't need to deny it." She gave him a shrewd look. "The thing is, Doctor, I have some, er, previous experience of such things."

He gave her a blank look, but didn't answer.

"No, I do. Look, if you don't believe me—and I can see that you are feeling, shall we say, reluctant?—why don't you call this man? He knows me well." She scrabbled in her bag for a pen and a piece of paper. "His name is Fielding Booker, and he's the captain of police in my hometown of Hamilton. He will be happy to give you my bona fides."

Dewey sat back triumphantly. Fielding Booker would have to agree, under the circumstances, that Dewey had often helped him with difficult cases. It might cost him a bit to admit it, but he would have to put aside his pride and come clean.

Little scratched his head and gave Dewey a wary look. There was a chance this lady, whoever she was, was right on the money. Because people didn't just die from eating salad dressing. Not in the ordinary course of things, no matter how allergic they were.

"Look," he said at last, "I'm not saying that you're right about this. But if, and I mean *if*, you're right, well, then I will be in your debt."

He rose, and Dewey did the same. "It isn't every day I get strangers in here giving me advice," he said, gesturing her toward the door. "But I wouldn't like it said that I left any stone unturned. And frankly, this thing is a puzzle. I'll see if your idea fits, Mrs. James. Thank you." He dismissed her and sat down once more at his desk.

After a few moments' thought, he reached for the telephone and dialed.

*   *   *

As usual, Larry Ceboll was eating when the telephone rang.

"Yeah," he said rudely, his mouth full of a baloney and onion sandwich. "Ceboll."

"Mr. Ceboll, sir, it's Packy Tate."

"Packy." Ceboll sighed. He sometimes wished Packy were a little less deferential. It got boring to feel so superior all the time. "What do you want?"

"Mr. Ceboll, I got something you maybe oughta know. For the newspaper."

"Right." Ceboll waited.

"Thing is, I had a call from Matt Little just now. You know that girl who died up there."

"Yeah, what about her?"

"I don't know, exactly. But Matt says he's gonna do another autopsy, because he isn't sure the first one got everything."

"I thought he already signed the certificate."

"Yup, he did. But now he's gonna look at that girl again."

"What's it mean, Packy?"

"Well, I don't know, rightly."

"Why the hell not?" Ceboll was angry. He didn't like to have his lunch disturbed by tomfoolery. If Tate had something to tell, that was one thing. But he ought to do his research first, and bother Larry Ceboll second.

"Well, because he wouldn't tell me. I asked, but he said he wasn't sure."

"Huh." Ceboll took the last bite of his sandwich and chewed loudly while he thought. "Any chance of getting a press pass to the show?"

"Uh, what show's that, Mr. Ceboll?"

"The autopsy show, Packy. Sounds to me like we've got something big."

"Yessir. That's how it seemed to me, anyway. I'm glad you see it like that."

"You call Matt Little for me, Packy, and find out what time he's gonna do this thing, and what he's looking for."

"Me call him?" Packy evidently felt he had done his job for Ceboll already.

"Yeah, Packy, you call him. And tell him—" Ceboll looked at his watch. "Tell him that six-thirty would be a good time."

"For what, Mr. Ceboll?"

"For him to tell me what the heck he's after." Ceboll slammed down the phone and reached for a can of luke-warm beer. He took a huge swallow, belched loudly, and then sat in quiet contemplation for a moment, an approximation of a smile on his thick lips.

Things were really looking up.

16

THE HOT, GARISH lamps of the examination room had been extinguished, leaving only pale shadows thrown by the fluorescent lighting in the corridor. Nyna-Joan Rebacker had gone home two hours ago, but Matthew Little had stayed on to finish his work. Now he sat at a small metal desk in the far corner of the examination room, making a few last notes in his log.

He had just completed a second autopsy report, and this one revised his earlier findings. He planned to drop it by Judge Hafter's house on his way home. It was likely that there would have to be an inquest of some sort, and the sooner they got on with it the better. Matthew Little didn't like what he had seen this afternoon.

On his second pass over the body of Harriet Bray, Little had found two things that had escaped his earlier notice. The first was a contusion to the back of the head; it was slight but noticeable, and he ought to have seen it the first time. But he had been blinded by the idea of the allergic reaction. Certainly the contusion was not the mark of a fatal blow, but likewise it was noteworthy. By the look of it, Harriet Bray had received a knock of sufficient strength to cause her to lose consciousness.

On the basis of this finding, Little began a minute inspection of the woman's body. And he found a second discrepancy, this one more alarming. The tissues of the larynx showed a slight bruising and faint lacerations, consistent with having swallowed a foreign object. Judging by the marks, Little estimated the object to have been narrowly cylindrical and fairly long. Something similar to a garden hose.

The conclusion was appalling.

Little had to admit that he was grateful to that James lady for pointing him in the right direction. Disturbing as his findings were, he infinitely preferred the truth to any comfortable misconceptions. It would have been extremely easy to chalk up the death as an accident, because of its freaky nature; there was not a doubt that the mustard had caused the young woman's death. But now it was looking more and more as though there had been nothing accidental about it.

The manner of her death would explain why she hadn't tasted the mustard. It would explain why such a persistently sensitive and cautious eater had consumed several table-spoons' worth of something to which she knew she was violently allergic. In light of what he now believed, Little would need to pay a visit to Judge Hafter, who served as county coroner for Edmunds and Villaseca. He glanced at his watch. The good judge would just about be getting home.

He closed his notebook, locked it in the drawer of the desk, and headed out.

Outside, under the tired branches of a dusty and sad-looking sycamore, Larry Ceboll was waiting in his pickup. The truck was a shiny black king cab with enormous tires and a tailgate covered with bumper stickers, most of them beer advertisements, but a few that sported boastful and offen-sive remarks about women. Ceboll liked the response he got from people who read his stickers. He especially enjoyed watching the little ladies scowl when they read some of the better ones. Larry Ceboll liked his little jokes.

Little hadn't called him, and there was no knowing if Packy Tate had delivered the message. Maybe he hadn't— Packy wasn't inclined to go that extra mile. That was okay, because Ceboll could make it look like a coincidence, running into him like this. He got out of the car and crossed the street just as Little was climbing into his old Chevy Malibu.

"Hi, Matt," said Ceboll.

Matthew Little was one of the few people in either Edmunds or Villaseca who could afford to snub Larry Ceboll. There were many who would have liked to, but nearly everybody in town owed him money, one way or another. Ceboll was quite generous with his loans, especially to tenants who fell behind on their rent. When they were just one day late, he would be there, offering terms on a delayed payment or a quiet cash loan at thirty percent a month. He had a sharp eye for business.

Little was immune. He had a county job and a successful private practice, he didn't need Ceboll's real estate, and he had a hefty savings account at the Villaseca National Bank. In spite of his immunity, however, he didn't like to snub anyone; his policy was to treat everyone with the same level of courtesy, because in life you just never knew. So he nodded politely to Ceboll and broke his stride to shake hands with him.

Little had the feeling Ceboll was after something, most likely news about the autopsy report. It never took Larry Ceboll long to sniff out the first hint of trouble. That idiot Packy Tate had probably been on the phone to him this afternoon, after he heard about the renewed autopsy request. Everyone in Edmunds knew that Packy Tate was one brick shy of a load, but generally speaking they didn't mind having a Barney Fife for a sheriff. Packy was more of an adornment than anything, because there weren't many serious crimes in Lincoln County. Parking-meter violations, drunkenness, and the occasional robbery were about the extent of wrongdoing—unless, of course, you counted Larry Ceboll's lifetime of extortion and loan-sharking. It would take more than a half-witted sheriff like Packy Tate to put Ceboll away.

It was true—there weren't usually many crimes in Edmunds. But Matt Little had the feeling, this evening, that he was looking at murder.

He wasn't about to let Ceboll in on it.

"Working late?" asked Ceboll, looking directly at the manila envelope in Little's hand. Larry Ceboll was nosy and didn't care who knew it.

Little casually shifted the envelope as he raised his arm to look at his watch. It was nearly seven. "Not too bad. I'll be home in time for the news. How've you been, Larry?"

"Good, good." Ceboll stifled a belch and hitched up his trousers. "We sold out of the *Trumpeter* this week."

"Did you now? Good to hear. Ad revenues up?"

"Well, not yet. Nobody knows, yet, that we're selling every copy. Once they know, they'll line up for space. That's why it's so important to keep hot stories going." Ceboll grinned, showing yellow teeth.

Little had seen the most recent issue of the *Trumpeter*. He thought the treatment of the Clearwaters was heavy-handed and perhaps libelous, but he didn't expect finer things from Larry Ceboll. "Well, that's what news hounds are best at, I guess," Little said ambiguously.

"Yeah. And speaking of news, Matt, I got a hunch there's something going on up there."

"Up where?" Little kept his face expressionless. He had

long ago learned the value of a poker face. Ceboll, however, didn't buy it.

"Aw, don't go giving me that servant-of-the-people bull, Matt." His tone was rude. "You know what I'm talking about." He pulled a stubby black cigar from his shirt pocket and began to fish around in his trousers pocket for a match. As he did so, he gestured casually toward the manila envelope. "Whatcha got in there, Matt?"

"Nothing to do with anything, Larry." Little gave him a courteous, vacant smile and opened his car door, which groaned heavily. He shook his head at the noise. "You know, my wife keeps suggesting we get rid of this car, but I sure love it." He patted the vinyl-clad roof. "More power than anything on the market these days. The only problem is finding good old-fashioned leaded gasoline."

"Yeah, well you can always go over the border for that."

"Good point," said Little, swinging neatly into the seat and shutting the door. He rolled down the window, and Ceboll leaned in.

"And while you're there, you might as well stock up on a few other old-fashioned things that ain't for sale around here." Ceboll chuckled at his witticism and lit his cigar.

Little gave him a look that might have been boredom, or might have been reproval. He didn't smile. "Been nice talking to you, Larry." The engine gave a roar, and Little peeled away in the direction of his house.

"Hot damn," said Ceboll.

He had been able to read the name on the envelope. It was addressed to Judge Nicholas Hafter, the county coroner.

Ceboll leaned against the fender of his truck, plotting his strategy. He would have to go carefully. This could be good, really good.

"You mean you just went and told him everything?" asked Gerald Clearwater. It was nearly eight o'clock. The rest of the guests were on the terrace under the magnolia, drinking their cocktails and talking over the events of the day; dinner would be served in fifteen minutes. Meanwhile, Gerald and Sonia were closeted with Dewey in the back room of the old stone outbuilding that served as the office building for Los Lobos.

Here, the twentieth century was in plain evidence—a fax machine, an espresso coffeemaker, a photocopier, and a wall lined with bookshelves and filing cabinets. The only antiques were the enormous oak desk and chair, in the mission style and probably two hundred years old. The desk had very likely served as a refectory table, or perhaps even an altar, Dewey reflected, as she looked around. Sonia had told her that this building had originally been used for food storage at the Hacienda; its thick stone walls had kept things relatively cool and fresh. Now it was a business office, discreetly tucked away from the guests.

Dewey had been quick to share her conclusion about Harriet Bray's death with her hosts. They had responded much as she had anticipated they would—with denial and disbelief. In the face of their outspoken reluctance to "stir things up," she had gone ahead on her own to talk to Matthew Little. She didn't expect them to appreciate it, but it had had to be done.

Now she was breaking it to them gently. Dewey had experience of these things, and she knew that the longer the misconception was allowed to persist, the worse it would be for everyone concerned.

Except the murderer, of course.

"Surely Dewey hasn't told him everything, Gerald." Sonia's words were calm, but she was tugging nervously at a great necklace of enormous faux pearls, wrapped double around her elegant throat. "You didn't tell him everything, did you, Dewey?"

"I'm not quite sure what you mean by everything, Sonia." Dewey was firm. "But I promise you that lingering rumors about that young woman's death would have done you no good. No good at all. I told him what I know and what I suspect."

Gerald was silent, and looked as though he were still trying to take it all in. Murdered—Dewey said the young woman had been murdered. But how could anyone be certain about that? If Matthew Little thought she had died from eating mustard, then how could her death have been anything other than an accident? Matthew Little was an excellent doctor. He wouldn't make a mistake about such a thing.

Sonia spoke. "I know that you're right, Dewey. Still, I can't help wishing—" She broke off.

"That we could just keep it under our hats?" Dewey was giving her old friend no quarter. This was a dreadful situation that must be faced, and the sooner Sonia relinquished her dreams of secrecy, the better. There was no keeping this matter quiet. And from a public-relations angle— which Dewey knew the Clearwaters were considering— it was far better for them to join noisily in the fray.

"Well, of course, if it really was—deliberate, I guess is the word—then of course we'd have to say something." Sonia didn't sound convinced. "It's just that—oh, I don't know. People are just sensitive about things like this."

"I should hope so, Sonia. And I think the word you want is *premeditated*. We're talking about murder, not a mismatched pair of bed sheets."

"What about the idea that it was just one of those crazy pranks, Dewey?" Sonia's voice held little hope. "Didn't you think it might be something like that?"

"It did cross my mind, Sonia. But look at the situation reasonably." She went back over her reasoning with them.

"If it was an accidental death, two conditions are necessary. First, that George mistakenly put mustard in the salad dressing and has subsequently forgotten doing so. Second, that Harriet Bray—who was constantly concerned about her health and preoccupied with her allergic condition— should so far have forgotten herself that she went ahead and ate the salad dressing, even though the taste of the mustard was extremely strong."

Sonia was silent for a moment. "Well, if you put it like that—but there must be another way of looking at it."

"This is the only logical way, Sonia. Surely you're not thinking that you could just ignore it."

"Oh, heavens, no. Of course not." Sonia looked shocked by the idea. "It's just that . . . well, I don't know. I suppose there is no *good* time for dealing with this kind of thing."

"No, you're right. There is no good time." Dewey was watching Gerald closely. He hadn't uttered a word since his first protest, but now he turned his robin's-egg-blue eyes toward Dewey.

She had once read something fanciful but persuasive about people with eyes of that particular shade of blue: They were reckoned to be the most believable liars ever born. Dewey had a sense about liars; still, she had known two really good, thoroughly credible ones in her time. By chance—or was it?—they both had had eyes of that robin's-egg blue.

"We'll just have to wait and see, Dewey," he said stiffly. "Right now, this is all the merest speculation."

"Yes, it is." Dewey regarded Gerald shrewdly. "But do you know, Gerald, I don't see how there can be any other explanation. Not if we accept the facts as we know them. Surely you don't think George is lying."

"Of course he doesn't," Sonia said quickly, covering the awkward pause that followed Dewey's question.

"And yet there is no doubt about the mustard. The obvious conclusion is that someone tampered with the dressing."

"But all we know is that someone added mustard, at some time," protested Gerald. "We don't know when or how. Perhaps Beverly did it, for some reason, and is now afraid to say so." Gerald sounded as though he almost believed it.

Dewey gave him a look: patience exasperated. "I won't argue with you further, Gerald," she said reasonably, "until we find out what Matthew Little has to say. I just wanted you to be forewarned, and thus forearmed."

If Dewey spoke with unusual formality and sternness, it was because she was dreadfully worried. If you looked at the situation, there was reason for alarm: not one dead girl at Los Lobos, but two. It would be just a matter of time before people began to look for connections, before the lingering uncertainties surrounding Monica Toro's death would once more be subject to interpretation—and misinterpretation.

"Sonia," said Dewey, in a thoughtful tone of voice, "have you told me everything about Monica Toro's death?"

"Monica?" The blood drained from Sonia's face, and she looked in alarm toward Gerald. He reached for a paper clip on the desk and began slowly to uncurl it.

"Honestly, Sonia." Dewey was impatient. "You don't think people will have forgotten, do you?"

"No," Sonia answered slowly, "of course not. It's just that—"

"I know. You and Gerald had a dreadful time over that. I understand, believe me, what it is to go through such an experience." She sighed. "From what I gather, there is still something unresolved about that whole affair." She cocked an eyebrow at Gerald. "Or am I wrong?"

"No, Dewey," Gerald replied, his voice full of hesitation. "You are certainly not wrong." The paper clip was now just a straight piece of wire. Painstakingly Gerald began to fold it again into its former useful shape. Dewey watched. Paper clips were never any good once you had straightened them. This was a fact of life.

Dewey waited, and at last Sonia spoke. "Monica's death was ruled an accident, Dewey, because there didn't seem to be any other explanation."

"But now?" Dewey prompted.

Sonia nodded. "Now, it all begins to look different. But the thing is, we can't imagine how it could have been anything other than an accident."

"Did you talk to Harriet Bray about it?"

"Yes," replied Sonia. "At length." She glanced sideways at her husband. "We both talked to her, because she was rather a friend of Monica's. Well—as much of a friend as Harriet could ever be. There was something a little bit off about her, you know. About Harriet, I mean."

"I wondered," said Dewey.

"She wasn't unlikable. She wasn't stupid. But she was awfully thick about people. She never seemed to understand them."

"How do you mean?"

"Well, she was full of innocent questions, like a little girl. She used to drive Sidney and Beverly nearly crazy, always asking them endless questions about what they were doing."

"You mean she was intrusive?"

"Not deliberately so," replied Sonia. "I mean, she would go into the kitchen and watch them stir the soup and say, 'Are you stirring the soup?' or something idiotic like that."

"Annoying." Dewey understood. She had thought that

Harriet might be a little bit strange that way. Innocently and endlessly curious about other people—about what they did, how they felt, how they got to be the way they were.

"How about the rest of the staff? You say Monica liked her?"

"Not exactly. They worked together, and they had a lot of interests in common. Poor thing—nobody liked her, really."

"But they put up with her," suggested Dewey.

"More or less. Charles, of course, was dreadful to her; he's perfectly awful to everyone, but terrific with our horses. That's just the way he is. Mark tolerated her kindly but stayed away from her. Sidney and Beverly used to banish her from the kitchen. But Monica was more or less of a friend."

Dewey sat deep in thought for a moment. "Then I suggest," she said to Sonia at last, "that we find out why this friendless young woman had to die. I have a feeling it was because her only friend died as well."

17

JUDGE NICHOLAS HAFTER was not an old man, but on the bench his wandering habit of speech and his occasional lapses into a drowsy state made him seem positively ancient. It was true that he wasn't really young anymore—he had seen fifty come and go, and then sixty—but he could still ride a horse, play three sets of tennis, and swim a mile in his backyard pool. He just seemed, when he wasn't engaged in athletic pursuits, like a semicomatose hick—it was something to do with the droop of his eyelids. The lawbreakers who had made the mistake of believing in this image had soon learned to regret it—as had the lawyers who had come before him in the Lincoln County Superior Court, where he had served as both criminal and civil trial judge for nearly forty years. Nicholas Hafter was nobody's fool.

He and Matthew Little were good friends; at times it seemed to the two of them that they were the only men in Lincoln County with an ounce of sense. Except of course for Gerald Clearwater; but Gerald, living halfway up a mountain and spending so much time at Los Lobos, didn't really count. He was isolated among his jet-setting clientele. When you came right down to it, he wasn't really one of them.

When Matt Little appeared at Hafter's door on that Thursday evening, it didn't take the judge long to understand the problem. After a quick look through the second autopsy report, Hafter nodded his head and agreed; the

young woman had been the victim of a particularly gruesome and obviously premeditated murder. The problem for
Hafter and Little was in how to cope with the facts.

The paying customers who came and went up at Los
Lobos were notoriously difficult, selfish, and vain. The
staff—with the exception of the local talent, in the form of
grooms and chambermaids—were likewise thorny. Sonia
and Gerald were hypersensitive about their image. Given all
these hindrances, bringing a full murder investigation to a
successful and swift conclusion would take diplomacy and
intelligence. Both of which, unfortunately, were in short
supply in Lincoln County, and altogether lacking in Sheriff
Packy Tate.

"It's his jurisdiction, Nicholas," said Little. "I don't really
know what we can do about it."

"Whatever we do, we can't put him in charge. He'll blow
the thing sky-high."

"And bring his buddy Ceboll in on it every step of the
way," concurred Little.

The judge thought for a moment. "If we could afford to
delay, I could ask the feds to bring a charge of violation of
the girl's civil rights."

"We can't wait on this. Somebody's been awfully clever."
Little shook his head in discouragement. It was clear that
there wouldn't be smooth sailing up at Los Lobos. Sonia
and Gerald, he knew, were still leery from the difficulties
following the accidental drowning of that other young
woman. Monica somebody or other. If their attitude the
other day had been any indication of what was to come,
Packy Tate would get nowhere.

"I think they'll stonewall, Nicholas," said Little. He
described his visit to the Hacienda and the scene in the
kitchen. "They still haven't told me which of their guests
made that salad dressing. Not that it really matters now."

"It could easily matter," responded Hafter. "Because you never know—that person could also have knocked her out and force-fed her the allergen."

"I suppose that's possible." He sighed. Sonia and Gerald would simply have to be more cooperative—or risk facing charges of obstruction of justice. "Maybe I can get that James lady to spill the beans."

"She's the one that came to see you?"

"That's right."

Hafter considered. "If Sonia and Gerald won't talk to you, there's no way on earth they'll talk to Packy."

"You don't have to tell me," Little replied warmly.

"So it seems to me that what we need is someone on the inside to help us." Hafter raised an eyebrow. "Like your little old lady."

The medical examiner chuckled. "I wouldn't describe her as a little old lady, exactly—but you're right. We need help. We need credibility up at Los Lobos. It's an interesting possibility."

"What do we know about her?"

"Well—after she left my office, I have to say I wondered about it. It seemed strange to me that she would just arrive out of the blue to tell me how to do my job."

"That kind of thing comes naturally to some people," quipped Hafter.

"True enough. Well, anyway, I was curious about her. So I called the police chief in her hometown and asked about her."

"What did he say?"

"I got the impression he thinks she's sort of a crackpot."

"Great."

"I know, it sounds bad. But he did tell me that she has kind of a reputation for sticking her nose into murder investigations. Now, I was reading between the lines, but it seemed to me that the police chief sees her as a rival."

"In other words, he wasn't complimentary."

"Not exactly. But he couldn't deny that she has helped him out once or twice."

Hafter considered in silence for a moment. "Okay, so she's helped her local chief of police with a murder investigation. That doesn't mean she's *not* a crackpot. Still, if he says she knows her stuff—well, then, that's a little bit different, I would guess. She from a small town?"

"The kind of place where everybody knows everybody."

"Sort of like Edmunds."

"More or less. I get the feeling it's not quite as dusty and hot."

"No place is as dusty and hot as Edmunds. All right. We know she might be able to help. So now the question is, do we let her in on it? Or just pump her for information, without telling her?"

"I somehow don't think we'd get away with that," replied Little. "I'd say there are no flies on her."

"Then we'll have to take her into our confidence."

"Think that'll be all right?"

"You tell me. You're the one that knows her."

"Well, she seemed sharp enough, that's for sure. Pretty determined. She told me she had come to see me on her own—I don't know whether she even consulted Sonia and Gerald about it at all."

"Hmmm." Hafter was thoughtful. "Can she manage Packy Tate?"

"Probably. Probably my three-year-old grandson could manage Packy Tate."

"Well, then. Why don't we go up there and talk to her?"

"Tomorrow morning suit you?"

Hafter reached inside his breast pocket and withdrew a

small leather diary, which he briefly consulted. "It will have to be early. I've got to be on the bench for the Swindles divorce at ten-thirty."

"They're finally getting their decree?" Little's eyes shone merrily. The Swindles had been threatening one another with divorce through nearly forty years of marriage; they were famous for it. Nobody in Edmunds believed they would ever go through with it, however. If the decree came through, it would be the end of a legend.

"That remains to be seen. I heard that the bookies are laying odds as to who doesn't show tomorrow."

"But I guess you'd better be there, for that one-in-a-million chance."

"It's a dog's life on the bench," said Hafter.

"Right, then." Little rose and gestured to the manila envelope. "I'll leave this copy of the report for you, in case you want to have another look at it before morning. And I'll pick you up at eight."

Little headed for the door, and Hafter accompanied him. "I hope your little old lady's not timid." He opened the door, and the two men stepped outside. The air was cool, and overhead the first stars were beginning to come out.

"No—definitely not," said Little. "Timid is definitely not the word for her." Little shrugged his shoulders. "I'm only worried that she might be a little too smart for her own good."

"How so? You mean she knows something more than she's telling?"

"No, I doubt it. If she were hiding something, I doubt she'd come to me. No—I just hope she knows how to look after herself, that's all." Little gave a wave and headed for his car. "I'll see you at eight," he called, over the groan of his car door.

*   *   *

Packy Tate, hiding behind an oak tree in Nicholas Hafter's next-door neighbor's yard, scratched his head thoughtfully. He didn't like the idea of being one-upped or made a monkey of. Hafter and Little were up to something, just like Mr. Ceboll suspected. Now, thought Packy Tate, it's time to find out what the heck is going on.

Larry Ceboll had called him, of course, with the news that the medical examiner had something in an envelope for the judge. Ceboll had asked him—or really, more or less told him—to go over to Hafter's place and find out what it was all about. Packy had waited outside in the chill April twilight for almost a half hour, finally to be rewarded with the sight of Little leaving the judge's house. He had only caught the tail end of the exchange between the two men, but that had been enough.

Ceboll had told Packy that there was something fishy about that girl, the one with the pink jumpsuits who died on Wednesday. Ceboll wanted to know what the medical examiner was telling the judge. Packy Tate agreed—because if Mr. Ceboll wanted to know, well, then Packy Tate wanted to know all about it, too. If there was something going on, they ought to tell Packy Tate about it. After all, Packy was the sheriff of this town. Sheriff of the whole county.

He got to Hafter's house too late to see Little arrive, so he had taken up his vigil in the shrubbery of the neighborhood. He had tried eavesdropping, but all the windows were shut tight, and there wasn't much cover right up close to the house. When Little left, he wasn't carrying any envelope, so Packy figured he must have left it inside—if he had brought it. Impossible to know for sure.

But at least he knew one thing: They were meeting at eight in the morning. That was pretty early, by Packy's standards, but he would just have to set the alarm and make sure he got out of bed in time. He was darned if he'd let them run rings around him.

He wondered now whether to follow Little some more, or knock on Hafter's door, or just call it a night.

In the end, he decided the best thing would be to check with Mr. Ceboll. He glanced at his watch. Just about eight. Mr. Ceboll would be heading for Molly's Foothill Paradise right about now, where he usually went for a couple of beers every night. Sheriff Packy Tate walked to the far end of the street, where he had parked his car behind a hedge in a side alley. He was proud of this precaution—at least he could be sure that Little and the judge hadn't spotted him. When you were doing undercover work, you couldn't be too careful.

The jukebox at Molly's Foothill Paradise was pretty good; the girls were better. That was why Larry Ceboll hung out there, and that was really why Molly's Foothill Paradise always did such a booming business. It was pretty far out on Route 17, and then you had to go along a dirt road for about a mile until you came to the big ramshackle building. But certain men in Edmunds and Villaseca were willing to make the trip almost nightly, to flirt with the girls and listen to the jukebox and watch whatever was on the TV over the bar.

Molly herself was in pretty good shape, if you considered she'd been running her bar for nearly thirty years. It was the kind of work that might have made some women look old, or like they'd seen too much, but Molly always looked pretty and fresh. Her waitresses all had to look pretty and fresh, too, or she'd get rid of them. There wasn't any room at her Paradise for girls with too much makeup, or girls with a hangover, or anything like that. They all wore little skirts and clean tops, no high heels, no tight jeans. They had to look like ladies, Molly said. It made the men feel better, and the men were the ones who counted, because they could really put away the beer. Beer was what Molly sold—beer and booze and nothing else. The girls were just a come-on. And they knew they had to behave themselves.

Packy Tate entered the place at about eight-thirty, and he quickly found Larry Ceboll perched on his favorite stool. He had one arm on the bar and the other around the neck of Ana María Perez, one of Molly's girls. Ana María tolerated Ceboll's sweaty arm because she knew there would be a decent tip at the end of the night, and that might mean she could get those new sneakers for her boy next week.

"Uh-oh, here comes the law," said someone at the bar. Molly looked up from behind the bar, gave Packy a nod, and went back to double-checking her receipts from yesterday. Ceboll slapped Ana María on the fanny, sending her away, and pulled up a bar stool for Packy, who made his way quickly through the unfamiliar smoky room. Packy Tate wasn't a regular at Molly's.

"C'mon, Sheriff, let me buy you a beer," Ceboll said in a loud voice. He gestured to Molly. "Two."

"Hi, Mr. Ceboll." Packy sat down, looking self-conscious, and glancing around him at the crowd. Most of the customers were people he knew only vaguely, although he could spot a few that had been in for drunk and disorderly once or twice. Packy did his best to look like one of the guys.

Molly arrived with two long-necked bottles and a glass for Tate. Ceboll threw a five-dollar bill on the bar. "You get the next ones. Well? What happened?" He grabbed a bottle and drank.

"Well, it was like you said," Packy told him, pouring beer into his glass. He glanced at Ceboll, drinking straight from the bottle, and then looked at his glass again, shrugging. "I went on over to Judge Hafter's place—"

"He see you?"

"Hunh-unh. No way. I kept way out of sight." He stopped pouring and let the foam settle.

"Good. What'd you see?"

Packy took a long swallow of beer, wiped his mouth, and continued. "They had some kind of a meeting."

"The envelope. Did you see it?"

"No, I didn't get a look at it. I think Matt Little must have left it there at the judge's house. He didn't have it with him when he came out."

"How long was he there?"

"Oh, about half an hour. Not long."

"Did you get close enough to find out what they were talking about?"

"No. I tried, but all the windows were shut, and besides he don't have real good bushes or anything right up close to the house."

Ceboll grunted, dissatisfied. "So we don't know anything, really."

"Oh, we know something, Mr. Ceboll. They got some kind of a plan. For tomorrow morning, at eight. I thought I'd tail them, find out what they're up to."

"They goin' somewhere?" Ceboll drained the last of his beer and showed his empty bottle to Tate, who fished in his pocket for money and signaled to Molly.

"Yeah, I heard Little say he'd be meeting the judge at his place. Pick him up."

"Okay, Packy, you follow them."

"What are you gonna do, Mr. Ceboll?"

Ceboll's expression grew wary. "Never you mind, Packy. What you don't know won't hurt you."

Molly arrived with more beer for Ceboll. Sheriff Tate

paid up and departed. If he was going to be getting up at the crack of dawn, he needed to be in bed.

In his small room at the end of the south wing, Charles Halifax lay on his bed, thinking.

He wasn't a man much given to contemplation; he was more accustomed to just doing what he pleased, whenever he felt like it. But things at Los Lobos had recently gotten out of hand. He needed to be in control again.

He was going to work out a plan that would edge him out of his present difficulties. With that idiot Harriet Bray out of the way, there should be smooth sailing ahead. Poor Harriet had just been a terrible loudmouth; that had been her great failing in life. Aside from her odious preoccupation with other people's health and fitness, she had had a knack for saying the wrong thing to the wrong people. Halifax supposed that it was too bad that she was dead—but really, when you came right down to it, who would miss her? Even Gerald and Sonia, who found a way to be nice to absolutely everyone, had been impatient with Harriet. Well, it had been impossible to like her, that was all.

Halifax put his arms up behind his head and crossed one ankle over a knee. His belly swelled and rolled with the movement, and his thigh muscles were surprisingly far from limber. He was fat, it was true. Well, now that Harriet wasn't around to watch, he could have just a piece of dry toast and black coffee for breakfast. He wouldn't miss the bacon and eggs, really, any more than he would miss that super-fit, loudmouthed, unfortunate woman.

18

THE NEXT MORNING, everyone at Los Lobos was up early. It was the last full day for the group—they would all leave early tomorrow—and for the most part they were glad their stay would soon come to an end.

Lorenzo and Serena were pleased with the insect life they had seen, and someday, they said, they would come back to make a full documentary of the place for "In the Field." But for now they were eager to be on their way, having laid open the secrets of the place to their scientific scrutiny. There were other insect worlds to be conquered, and the sooner the better.

The Miltons had just plain had enough, and they made no bones about it. Belinda, taking her morning coffee under the magnolia, went so far as to say so.

"You can have this kind of vacation, as far as I'm concerned," she said heavily. She reached for a warm, freshly baked baguette from the basket on the table in front of her. She broke off a piece and spread homemade quince jam on it, and the aroma of the hot bread and the jam wafted deliciously up into the sunlit morning air. "I mean, it's been okay, but it's too expensive for what they give you. At least if you go on a cruise, the scenery changes every day. Here you're just sort of stuck."

George flashed a quick look of amusement Dewey's way. Not everyone could appreciate the mastery of three meals a day prepared by Sidney Bachelor, nor the unique quality of the setting and the furnishings. George Farnham liked a good cruise as much as anyone, but Los Lobos had distinctive charm and an allure all its own.

"Plus," Philip Milton intoned moodily, "I think it's enormously prejudicial to be in a place where somebody died."

"Prejudicial to what?" asked George, in his most lawyerly tone of voice.

"Prejudicial to enjoyment," answered Belinda. "I'm beginning to think there *are* ghosts at this joint."

"What are your plans for today?" Dewey asked politely, to change the subject. She really didn't enjoy listening to people complain. Life was just too short to be so negative, especially with these delicious hot baguettes of Sidney's right here on the table. Honestly, some people were just born to whine. She spread a thick layer of jam on a piece of the crusty bread. "Do you and Philip have an activity scheduled?"

"Um, I think we're going out on horses this morning." Belinda talked with her mouth full. "Up to the laguna, with that fat guy."

The fat guy, Dewey assumed, was Charles Halifax. She noticed that he had made himself rather scarce since Harriet's sudden death. Perhaps it had spooked him. Or perhaps there was something else. Dewey had noticed how Charles loathed Harriet, but he seemed to detest everyone equally. "And you?" she asked, turning to the Lees.

Lorenzo responded with his usual enthusiasm. His eyes shone with excitement. "Oh, we've found an absolute *gem* of an ant lion trap. It's about two miles or so up along in the valley. Haven't we, dear?" He gave his wife an affectionate glance. "We're going to film it and photograph it all day. It will be most interesting to see who falls in."

"How very amusing," murmured Eloise Morningside.

"George here has promised me a game of tennis. Haven't you, George?"

"That's right," assented George, nodding heartily. "We're going to have a game."

"I'll just bet you are," said Belinda Milton, in a whisper loud enough for Dewey to hear.

"Are you a good player?" Serena asked George politely, oblivious to undercurrents.

"Oh, I guess you might say I can hold my own. Don't play as much as I'd like, generally, but I've always found it invigorating. I'd like to play more often. Maybe from now on I'll be more inspired to get out there." He pantomimed a backhand crosscourt shot.

Dewey suddenly and inexplicably began to feel left out. She had quite an agreeable plan for the morning—Sonia had promised to let her browse through the Hacienda's library, which included some very fine, rare editions on the history of the area and the adventures of the people who had settled the Escondida Valley. Still, she suddenly wished she were going somewhere on horseback with the Miltons, or even going out to look at ant lions with the Lees. She didn't feel like being on her own. She quickly finished her coffee, gathered up her large handbag, and headed for the library.

This was a small room next to the red parlor, lined with bookshelves and fitted out with a small desk and a few exquisitely comfortable, velvet-covered armchairs. She quickly discovered Great-uncle Horacio's diary, which proved to be exceptionally interesting. The man had had a sense of humor, and—for a bandit—he had been considerably humane in the treatment of his victims. It was under his guidance that most of the present-day house had been constructed, and with flair befitting an imaginative bandit, he seemed to have outfitted the place with all kinds of unexpected hiding places, cleverly disguised hollow areas

in the walls, trapdoors in the floors. Dewey wondered if
there was still some treasure hidden away somewhere. Some
rare gold coins, perhaps. Or, more likely, two-hundred-year-
old beef jerky, stolen from a passing caravan of covered
wagons.

Lost in Great-uncle Horacio's world, Dewey didn't hear
the door to the library open.

Matthew Little and Nicholas Hafter stood on the thresh-
old. Little cleared his throat, and Dewey looked up.

"Oh! Good morning, Dr. Little," said Dewey, somewhat
flustered.

"Didn't mean to startle you, Mrs. James," he said politely.
The two men entered the room, and Hafter was introduced.

"We've come to ask your assistance, Mrs. James," said
Little, "in a most serious matter."

"Oh?" Dewey was instantly alert. She had been waiting
for this, she realized. Perhaps that would account for her
anxiety at breakfast.

Little took a seat opposite Dewey; Hafter leaned up
against the wall and glanced casually out through the
window to the apricot orchard beyond. It was a beautiful
morning.

"On the strength of your visit to me the other day," said
Little, "I went back and performed a second autopsy on that
young woman." He adjusted a trouser leg, crossed his feet at
the ankles, and gave her a somber look.

"And?" Dewey felt sure what the response would be.

"You were right, Mrs. James. There were clear signs that
the death was not the result of a simple allergic reaction,
although that reaction definitely took place."

"What was her death the result of, then, Doctor?"

Little glanced at Hafter. "Based on the evidence I saw
yesterday, I would have to conclude that her death was not
accidental."

"I thought as much," Dewey said softly.

Hafter spoke up. "Naturally, in the face of the allergic reaction, Dr. Little's original conclusion was completely understandable."

Dewey nodded her agreement. "Naturally." She looked thoughtful. "In other words, the allergic reaction was used to mask the traces of more deliberate activity."

Little scratched his chin. "That seems to be the conclusion we've reached." He cocked an eyebrow at Dewey. "Do you want the details?"

"Oh—yes, I suppose so."

Little spelled out the grim findings of the second autopsy for her.

"Ye gods," Dewey said softly, as the dreadful implications came home to her. She had been right, but that knowledge was a burden. She had felt it was right to insist on another investigation, but the facts suddenly seemed more gruesome than she had anticipated. "What a perfectly cold-blooded and horrible thing to do."

"We thought so." Little's voice was dry, his tone cool and matter-of-fact.

Judge Hafter nodded. "Matt came to see me last night, and I took a look at the autopsy report myself. Not that I've had a great deal of experience of such things—we don't have many murders here in Edmunds, thank heaven, so I'm no expert. But it's my duty to issue a coroner's report on this matter, and I have already told Matt that I find this is certainly murder. I'm ready to issue that finding this morning, which will authorize the local law-enforcement agencies to open a full investigation into the matter."

Dewey looked at the two men. It was evident that they had come to her with a specific purpose in mind. She could only guess at what they wanted—information about Sonia and Gerald. Her mind flew to last month's fatal accident, and she wondered briefly if, in the light of the new facts about Harriet's death, these two men had considered it. It was odd that two young women should die here, within such a short space of time.

Suddenly Dewey began to feel terribly uneasy. She had seen this kind of thing before—in Hamilton, she had even helped Captain Fielding Booker to get to the bottom of one or two mysterious deaths—but never before had she felt so worried. Something seemed to strike very close to home. Suddenly, for the first time in her life, she wasn't sure, at all, that she should have stirred the pot.

But of course she had had no choice. One never had a choice in such circumstances—one merely did what was right.

She looked Judge Hafter straight in the eye. "Have you got a suspect in mind, Judge?"

Hafter shook his head. "Frankly we haven't got a clue." He glanced toward Little, then continued. "The thing is, Matt found Sonia and Gerald sort of difficult to talk to the other day. He was surprised when you came to see him, and at first of course he was a bit skeptical, but it seems your suspicions were right on the button. Which just goes to show that you're paying attention, and that you're an objective witness to what's been going on up here."

Dewey started to remonstrate, but thought better of it. Despite her friendship with Sonia and Gerald, she *was* objective. Hadn't she gone straight to the medical examiner with her suspicions?

Hafter went on. He explained, in the most diplomatic terms he could muster, what an idiot Packy Tate was. Dewey quickly understood, without being told, that he couldn't be turned loose on the people at Los Lobos. Not if they hoped to find the murderer.

"We think, ma'am, that you might be able to help us

further," Little put in, when Hafter had outlined the situation. "What we need is background information on all of the staff, and probably on the guests as well. The principal thing we need to know is who disliked Harriet Bray, and why."

"That one is simple," said Dewey.

"Why?"

"Well, because the poor thing seems to have been universally disliked."

"Oh." Little looked disappointed. "Had a nasty streak, did she?"

"Oh, no. Rather the reverse, I'd say. The kind that wouldn't hurt a fly. Just a natural-born talker. It was difficult to get her to be quiet—she always had *something* to say on a subject. She was very like a child."

"Then why would anybody murder her?" asked Little.

"I doubt she really could have been as harmless as all that," seconded Hafter.

"People like that often get themselves into trouble," Dewey pointed out. "They don't mean to be offensive, but they step on toes quite easily, plunging in with too much enthusiasm and saying the wrong thing."

"You don't get yourself murdered for making a faux pas," objected Hafter. "Nor for being the biggest bore in town."

"No," agreed Dewey, "you don't. But Harriet's failing was that she utterly lacked discretion. I'm willing to wager that she said something in the wrong company—and whatever it was she said, it got her killed."

"But what could she possibly have said?" objected Little.

"That's what we'll need to find out," responded Dewey. She looked at the men thoughtfully. "Has it struck you," she asked, "that there are two young women dead?"

Hafter looked quizzically at Little, who began to nod. "The girl who drowned up here."

"That's right," said Dewey. "Harriet Bray worked closely

with that young woman, Monica. Don't you think that it's a mighty strange coincidence?"

"I suppose it seems like one too many, at least," said Little. "Or maybe two too many."

"That's it exactly." Dewey raised an eyebrow, and her blue eyes reflected her earnestness.

"You think the two deaths are related, then?"

"Well, it certainly comes to mind. Doesn't it?"

Little considered the point.

"Wait a minute, Mrs. James," said Hafter. "You mean you think that other girl was murdered, too?" He sounded incredulous. Maybe Little had come up with a little old lady who saw homicidal maniacs on every corner. There were plenty of little old ladies like that, Hafter knew. Thankfully, there weren't many in Lincoln County.

"Well, it is one possibility. You have to see that, Judge."

Little nodded, and his eyes held a flash of interest; he was considering the point carefully. At last he spoke.

"I see what you mean, Mrs. James."

"I'm not sure I do," protested Hafter.

"Don't think me paranoid, Judge," Dewey said soothingly. "But you must admit that it's odd. And if there is one murder—well, it stands to reason that any other sudden death must be looked into fully."

Little agreed. "If you think about it, that's a reasonable motive for wanting this girl out of the way—that she knew something about the drowned girl." He thought for a moment more, then shook his head. "There's only one problem there," he said finally. "I did the exam on that girl myself. She definitely drowned."

Dewey hesitated to point out the obvious. "If you'll forgive my mentioning it, Dr. Little," she said meekly, "you also examined Harriet Bray."

"Agreed—but that was different," said Hafter, coming to

Little's defense. "The singularity of the anaphylactic reaction was so strong as to be overwhelmingly the probable cause of death. And in fact the reaction did occur."

"But isn't that true, too, about Monica Toro? When you find a young woman in a swimming pool, with her lungs filled with water, I believe it's only natural to assume that the victim has drowned. The thing is, we don't know why she drowned."

The two men were silent, and Dewey's voice was suddenly hard. "There are two possibilities. She may have met with an accident—a cramp, or what have you—or someone may have held her head underwater until she was dead."

There was a silence while the men contemplated the vision of the young woman, struggling against someone stronger, someone with a lethal advantage over her.

Dewey glanced down at the diary of Great-uncle Horacio, which had fallen open in her lap. It seemed that life in the Escondida Valley could still be savage today. She gave the men a shrewd look.

"If you'll forgive my intruding my opinion into something that really doesn't concern me, I suggest that this is where the search will have to start. With the events of last month, here at Los Lobos."

19

Nyna-Joan Rebacker didn't have much experience with hangovers, but when she awoke that morning she knew for certain that she had one. She also knew who had given it to her. Larry Ceboll.

He'd called her last night, out of the blue. He always called if he wanted something, never any other time. He'd suggested that he would like to see her—they were old friends, and had been high-school sweethearts after all. Nyna-Joan made an excuse to her husband and left the house to rendezvous at nine-thirty with Larry. Not that she needed to excuse herself to her husband—he was always sound asleep in the recliner chair by nine-fifteen, with the Home Shopping Network on the television. He always fell asleep before buying anything, which was just as well. They didn't have much money to spare.

Nyna-Joan had climbed in the pickup and slipped away to Molly's Foothill Paradise. There Larry had filled her with beer and tequila and tales of his derring-do—he was quite a storyteller when he wanted to be. In fifteen minutes Nyna-Joan Rebacker was laughing and laughing. After her second shot of tequila, she wanted to be as entertaining as Larry was. By the time she'd had her fifth shot of tequila and her third beer, Nyna-Joan Rebacker had spilled the beans.

There really hadn't been much to tell, but Larry held out the promise of three hundred dollars, so Nyna-Joan had told

not only what she knew, but also what she imagined or
suspected. She performed a creditable imitation of Dewey
James arriving at the County Medical Examiner's office,
mimicking with skill the prim way Dewey had sat in the
waiting room. With that, Nyna-Joan made Larry Ceboll
laugh, which was the one thing she could do that almost
nobody else in Edmunds could do.

For sentimental reasons, Larry was inclined to be generous with his old flame. One hundred and fifty dollars had
come her way last night—plus, Larry had paid for all the
drinks. The other one-fifty would be hers with a copy of the
second autopsy report. That would be easy, because Dr.
Little only came to the county office twice a week. Today
was one of his days in his own office, at his house.
Nyna-Joan would have the run of the place, and she had
promised that Larry could have the copy by eight o'clock.

This morning she was feeling a little bit guilty about what
she had told Larry, but only a little. It didn't seem to her that
there was any reason not to tell him—after all, the County
ME records were supposed to be public anyway. Once the
report was finalized, it would go in the records file, and Dr.
Little worked fast. If you thought about it, Nyna-Joan was
only advancing things by a day or so. She knew enough
about the forensic law of Lincoln County to know that. So
she shrugged off her sense of guilt, climbed out of bed, and
got herself ready for work.

What Nyna-Joan didn't know was that Larry Ceboll had
already acted on the information she had given him. After
leaving Molly's, he had gone straight to Packy Tate's house
to discuss the situation, rousing the sheriff from his innocent
sleep to plan his strategy. He told Tate all about the old lady
from Los Lobos who had come to see Little yesterday and
talked him into doing a second autopsy. Nyna-Joan had,
naturally, listened to every word exchanged between them,

and she had reported on the conversation fully. Plus, she had seen the preliminary notes for the second report. It sounded to Ceboll like Little was building a case.

"And they're doing it behind your back, Packy. Without even discussing it with the law. Come on, Packy, stick up for yourself. Hell, man, you're the sheriff of Edmunds and Villaseca and all of Lincoln County. Yet they just think they can do whatever they want, without consulting you. Now, how does that make you feel?"

Packy had admitted sleepily that it made him feel pretty low. So he and Ceboll had hatched a new plan, and with the help of Judge Baker, who owed Larry big money, they had completed all the necessary paperwork at eight-fifteen the following morning—right after Nyna-Joan had come by the *Trumpeter* office with the report.

Now Packy Tate was slumped way down in the driver's seat, on a stakeout. He had parked his conspicuously marked car way off the side road into Los Lobos, so nobody would see him. Sonia and Gerald had driven by about fifteen minutes ago—they always went into town on Friday mornings, to go to the bank and run a few errands and get payroll matters sorted out. You could always count on them for that. With the Clearwaters safely out of the way, this would be a piece of cake. Mr. Ceboll had instructed Packy just to wait until Hafter and Little left, and then to proceed.

Sheriff Packy Tate's patience was soon rewarded. By nine-thirty, Little and Hafter had finished their conference with Dewey. Tate pulled down the visor of the baseball cap that concealed his eyes and watched as Little's car made the turn onto Route 31, heading back down into Edmunds. Then he made his move.

After her visitors had left, Dewey had found her mind far too preoccupied to continue with her reading. She put

Great-uncle Horacio's diary away on the shelf and went outside for a walk.

It was second nature for her to make her way to the stables, where she looked forward to being soothed by the wordless company of Soda Pop, Monkey Boy, and Pumpkin Pie. Carlitos was there, overseeing the shoeing of Cerveza's near forefoot, and they talked of horses and this and that, until Dewey's mind had stopped racing. Carlitos was expansive on the subject of the breeding business, which had recently suffered a few setbacks. Dewey learned that Cerveza was to have been sold, but the deal had fallen through at the last minute.

"He's a beautiful horse," said Carlitos, "and already his children are winning races in Brazil. I don't know what happened."

"Perhaps the buyer had a change of heart," said Dewey. Something about this matter rang a bell. It had to do with the papers she had glimpsed on Charles Halifax's desk, three days ago.

Ye gods, had it only been three days? It felt like months since she had started out on this venture. She listened politely as Carlitos related some more interesting facts about Cerveza, but her mind kept straying to the strange goings-on at Los Lobos. If this kind of thing kept up, there would be no way that Sonia and Gerald would be able to hang on to the place.

Dewey suddenly realized something that should have been obvious days ago. Since Harriet's death, there had been no more notes from "Monica." Dewey's absorption in the murder had caused her to forget all about the Los Lobos ghost—but now she was struck by the coincidence, and suddenly quite sure that it wasn't a coincidence at all. But she couldn't be certain what it signified. She couldn't even be certain that it was important, or germane to the matter at hand. She needed to talk to George, to think things through aloud. But he was off on the tennis court with Eloise Morningside. She wondered what the score was.

"Morning, Carlitos," said an unfamiliar voice.

"Good morning, Sheriff," said Carlitos, hardly bothering to nod.

Dewey looked with curiosity. This must be Packy Tate, the sheriff who had gotten on Gerald's nerves so badly. The one that Little and Hafter were trying to circumvent. Dewey felt a sudden knot in the pit of her stomach. Had he come to question Gerald yet again?

"Excuse me, ma'am," Packy Tate said deferentially. An abrupt insecurity had overtaken him. This was the person that Little and Hafter had their secret rendezvous with? This was the object of Mr. Ceboll's elaborate plan? Maybe he was mistaken. "Um, excuse me, but are you, um, Dewey James?"

"I am," said that lady. "You must be Sheriff Tate. I've heard a great deal about you. I'm very pleased to meet you." She stuck out a hand to shake.

Packy Tate was now deeply confused and uncertain. There was nothing in his experience to help him with this one. Did you shake somebody's hand and then take them in? Or did you take them in first, and then shake hands? He scratched his head for a minute, and at last he decided to ignore the hand altogether. It was just too confusing.

He reached in his breast pocket and pulled out an impressive-looking document. "Dewey James," he intoned, "I have here a warrant for your arrest in connection with the murder of Harriet Bray."

20

GEORGE FARNHAM AND Eloise Morningside finished their second set of tennis and walked slowly back toward the main house. They were just in time to see Sheriff Tate's car head out along the back road out of Los Lobos, with Dewey perched upright in the backseat. As Tate made his way to the back entrance, Sonia and Gerald were arriving through the main gates.

"Grand Central Station," commented Eloise. "If I'm not mistaken, the car going out the back way was the long arm of the law. I wonder what's going on?"

"Good question," said George, unsure of how much to divulge. Nobody here—except Sonia and Gerald, he supposed—knew that murder was suspected, and Dewey probably wouldn't appreciate his letting the cat out of the bag. Undoubtedly she had decided to confide her suspicions to the local sheriff. That was to be expected. "Good question."

"But George, wasn't that Dewey James in the back?" pursued Eloise, her voice throaty and confidential. "I wonder what she can be doing with the sheriff?"

George grinned. "Well, she's the kind of person who's always up to something."

"Really." Eloise sounded disbelieving. Perhaps she didn't imagine that a retired librarian was the type to get up to things. "Well, I guess then that the sheriff has found out about her at last and taken her in."

George chuckled. "That'll be the day. No—the thing about Dewey is that she positively loves policemen—her late husband was the captain of police in Hamilton. She's probably being given a personal tour of the local jail."

"How quaint." Eloise was dismissive. They had reached the main building and found Sonia and Gerald on the front porch, in the thick of a loud altercation with the groom, Carlitos. The discussion went forward in rapid Spanish, but even without understanding a word, George could tell there was something relatively important going on. Carlitos was gesturing wildly, pointing a finger now at Sonia, now at Gerald. The Clearwaters in their turn were apparently flabbergasted by what he was telling them.

"Now what?" Eloise asked in a bored voice. "This place is really getting peculiar." She gave her silky hair a toss and adjusted the stylish bandanna at her throat. "One of the staff seems to have got himself in trouble with the management. Dear me."

"It certainly looks that way," George agreed. He was mildly curious; something important was undoubtedly going on. Sonia looked rather desperate. She caught sight of George and summoned him urgently; he excused himself to Eloise and joined the group on the porch.

As Eloise headed off toward the west wing, she heard Sonia's frantic exclamation to George. "That idiot Packy Tate," Sonia said savagely. "He's gone and arrested Dewey."

George looked at Carlitos, and then back at Sonia. "Now, Sonia, I'm sure that's not right."

"It is right, George. Carlitos says that stupid, stupid man came here with a warrant. He snuck in here while we were down in Edmunds at the bank—he knew perfectly well we wouldn't be here. Ooh! I have a mind to sue him."

"Calm yourself." George nodded discreetly in Carlitos's

direction. Obviously, this old man had misunderstood. "Perhaps we've had a misinterpretation of the facts," he said gently. "Dewey's always going off with policemen. You know that as well as I do. I'm sure she just found a way to interrogate him. You know how she is."

"No, sir." Carlitos was polite but absolutely firm. He gave an amused glance at George, whose surprise was evident. "Yes, I do speak English."

"Sorry," said George, flustered.

"No apology necessary." Carlitos waved a hand. "Shall I tell you what happened?"

"Please."

Carlitos embarked once more upon his tale. Sonia and Gerald, who had heard it already, listened with impatience.

According to Carlitos, Packy Tate had arrived at about nine-thirty, bearing a warrant signed that morning by Judge Baker.

"That man Baker is the biggest crook in Edmunds," interjected Gerald, indignant. "The man bought the election last year."

"Hush, Gerald," said Sonia. She agreed with him about Baker; but this was not the time or place. "Go on, Carlitos."

Carlitos continued with his story. The warrant named her as a material witness in the investigation into the murder of Harriet Bray, and she was to be detained in the sheriff's custody pending a further decision by the judge.

Dewey naturally had been surprised, but according to Carlitos she had seemed more curious than worried. She had readily accepted the invitation and climbed unhesitatingly into the sheriff's car.

"This is all my fault," Sonia said mournfully. "Dewey's in jail because of me."

"I won't disagree with you there," replied George, but his voice was kind. "Now, let's stop blaming ourselves and get her out. Assuming they've managed to incarcerate her, which they probably haven't. Knowing Dewey, she has no doubt found a way to talk rings around the sheriff. He's probably the one in jail. Gerald, we need to get to town right away."

Gerald's eyes had their customary faraway, daydreaming look, but he spoke precisely. "You're right about that, George." He turned to the groom. "Thank you for telling us about this, Carlitos. I think I may need you to help us with this. Go tell Charles that he'll have to do without you this morning."

Carlitos nodded and headed for the stables. Gerald turned to Sonia. "You stay here with our guests, my dear. George and I will go. Carlitos can drive us."

"I will not stay here and let my dear friend languish in prison."

"Sonia, for heaven's sake, don't be so overly dramatic. Please, stay here."

"No, Gerald."

George spoke up. "Enough squabbling, you two. Listen. This is a delicate situation. Dewey suspected murder, and obviously the sheriff is in agreement. You had better keep your heads down, both of you, if you want to get through this as smoothly as possible. Besides, you have your other guests to think of, and if Dewey has actually been arrested it may take all day to get her out. I'll go by myself."

Sonia protested. "But you don't know anybody in Edmunds. That's absurd, George."

"All I need is a local attorney, because I'm not licensed to practice here. Not that we'll get to that stage—there must be some misunderstanding, that's all. I'm sure there's a lawyer in Edmunds who'll help me."

"I doubt it," said Sonia. "There are only two, and they're

both in Larry Ceboll's pocket. You just know this *had* to be his idea." She was scornful.

Gerald gave them a dreamy look. "Sonia, what about the young one with the immigration practice? Has a little storefront on Santa Maria."

"Excellent suggestion." Sonia turned to George. "He'll help. His name is Steven Shinefeld, and he's very nice. He also seems to have no fear of Larry Ceboll."

"All right. Can someone take me to town?"

"Carlitos will drive you," said Sonia. "He seems to be quite taken with our dear Dewey. He's terribly worried about her."

"He needn't worry, tell him," said George. "Dewey is one gal who knows how to take care of herself."

In two hours, the process of extracting Dewey from jail was nearly complete. As Sonia had said, Steven Shinefeld was a very nice young man, and delighted to help. He was good-looking, lithe, about twenty-eight or -nine, with dark hair, deep blue eyes, and a lively manner. His office was a small storefront, as described, but to George it seemed like a storefront with a difference. There were handsome prints on the walls, and a small but beautifully maintained legal library in the back. Shinefeld was wearing jeans, a black shirt, and a turquoise and silver western-style clasp on his bolo tie. George thought there might be some benefits to practicing in a town like Edmunds. The dress code, for example.

Shinefeld welcomed George's request with enthusiasm. "My work tends to be a little repetitive," he commented, "so I leap at everything. Plus, it's good to work with a different type of client. Keeps me on my toes."

Steven Shinefeld knew the local bond procedures inside and out. George agreed to put up a guaranty should one be needed, and within half an hour the preliminaries had been taken care of. They left the little office on Santa Maria and headed toward the courthouse, about half a mile down on the left.

"Packy Tate is a fool," the young lawyer commented to George, as they walked briskly along the sidewalk toward Judge Hafter's courtroom. "But on his own, he's totally innocuous. Obviously Ceboll put him up to this."

"Who is this Ceboll character? He own this town?"

"More or less," Shinefeld agreed. "Not only this one but Villaseca, too, the next town over. All the commercial real estate, the local newspaper, and half the public officials. Probably more."

"Why do they put up with him?"

"Everybody's scared of him. He's got promissory notes signed by about a third of the population—and probably worse things on some of the others."

"How come you're not afraid of him?"

Shinefeld shrugged. "I don't know. He's just a buffoon, it seems to me."

"Not a dangerous man?"

"Well—it depends on your point of view. He's probably dangerous to Gerald Clearwater. He wants Los Lobos."

"He wants to buy it?"

"Well, he'd like to get it for free. Or by default somehow. But yeah, he would buy it. Wants to develop it. He told me that the first thing he'll do when he gets his hands on it is tear down the chapel and put up some luxury condos. Swell guy."

"I get the picture." They had reached the courthouse, a small, one-story wooden building surrounded by dusty-looking oak trees. Shinefeld held the door open for George.

"Room Three—Judge Nicholas Hafter. I'm hoping we can get him to rescind the warrant."

"Is he a reasonable man?"

"Very. And he has no use for Packy Tate. He'll be eager to help."

They met Hafter in the hallway, getting a breath of air after dealing with the legendary Swindles divorce. The decree wasn't going through; Philo Swindle had changed his mind, and the happy couple were even now embracing in the courtroom.

"You're not on my docket for today," he told Shinefeld, "but we'll make time in chambers, if you like. I have a drunk and disorderly, then I'm free." He glanced at his watch. "Say, twenty minutes."

Half an hour later, George emerged from Judge Hafter's chambers, clutching in his hand the order to rescind the warrant. Hafter had been furious when he heard the tale of Dewey's detention and vowed to start a campaign to impeach both Packy Tate and Judge Baker. In the meantime, he gave George strict instructions not to discuss the investigation with anyone. "Not even with Mrs. James," he admonished. "We don't want to create grounds for any further activity on the part of Packy Tate. Tell Mrs. James for me that she can call if she runs into any kind of problem."

George thanked Hafter, and they departed. Carlitos had brought the car around and was waiting out front; he drove them out to Packy Tate's office, where poor Dewey was cooling her heels in the small cell at the back.

Tate was sitting on the far side of the large room, behind a big gray metal desk, pretending to be busy with some paperwork. He glanced up and nodded as the three men entered his office. "Morning. Be with you in a minute," he said, trying to sound casual.

Shinefeld strode easily up to the desk and plonked down

the order signed by Judge Hafter. "Packy, what did you think you were doing?" he asked, his voice friendly.

Tate glanced at the order. "Mr. Shinefeld, I'm real busy right now."

"No you're not," Shinefeld said gently. He reached across the desk and grabbed Tate by the collar. "I suggest you take a look at the order to rescind," he said, his voice still quiet and friendly, "before I have to make a citizen's arrest."

"Now, just a minute," said Packy, anxious. "I'm not going to fall for these tricks."

Shinefeld released his grasp. He could tell by Tate's expression that the deal was done. "Open the cell door now, Packy, and let her out. This is a legal instrument—unlike that phony baloney that you and Ceboll and Baker cooked up."

"That was legal," whined Packy, fishing nervously in his desk for the key to the lockup.

"Don't be ridiculous. That wasn't worth the paper it was written on, and you know it."

Packy hung his head.

"Let her out," repeated Shinefeld.

"Okay," said Packy, "okay, all right." He disappeared through the door at the back of the room and reappeared moments later with Dewey.

She didn't appear any the worse for wear, and was grateful to see George and Carlitos, who were both solicitous of her well-being. "Good heavens, I'm perfectly fine," she said rather impatiently, when George asked her for the fifth time how she was. "Perfectly fine. It's a nice clean cell, much better than the one Fielding Booker has in Hamilton. I must speak to him about it. Quite comfortable indeed."

She gave Shinefeld a glance. "I imagine I'm in your debt, somehow."

"Not at all," demurred Shinefeld, introducing himself. "I was pleased to help."

Dewey turned to Sheriff Tate. "Well, now," she said airily, "that was an interesting interlude. *Most* interesting. I might even go so far as to call it a strange interlude. I thank you for your hospitality, Sheriff." She bowed to him.

"Aw, Mrs. James, now listen——"

Dewey held up a hand. "It's perfectly all right. Don't worry, I'm not going to press charges against you for false arrest."

"False arrest!" Packy Tate exclaimed.

"You should," George interjected. He glowered at Tate. "I'm her lawyer, and I'm going to see that she does it."

"No, I don't think I need to press charges, George." Dewey shook her head. "Besides, Mr. Shinefeld is my lawyer." She smiled at him. "No, there will be no need to press charges—not as long as we get to the bottom of this strange interlude. I imagine that there is more to this than meets the eye." She turned her gaze on Tate. "For example—who, Sheriff, is Mr. Ceboll?"

George and Shinefeld exchanged glances; Packy Tate shuffled his feet and looked miserable.

"Who is he?" Dewey repeated. "I heard you talking to him on the telephone not five minutes after we arrived. 'Okay, Mr. Ceboll, she's here,' you said. I presume you were speaking of me."

Packy Tate was silent.

"You don't have to answer," said Dewey. "We'll work it out." She nodded to the sheriff, put her arm through Carlitos's, and sailed majestically through the door. George and Shinefeld followed.

21

"Now, CARLITOS," SAID Dewey, as they came out into the sunshine, "where do I find the mysterious Mr. Ceboll?"

Carlitos opened the car door, and Dewey climbed in the front seat. George and Shinefeld got in the back, and Carlitos turned the car toward Edmunds. "He's in town, Mrs. James. He runs the *Trumpeter*, and the office is right on Santa Maria, downtown."

"Then let's go there, please, and on the way you can tell me all about him."

Carlitos obliged. He told Dewey everything he knew about Larry Ceboll—about his bottomless greed, his disgusting manners, his oafish behavior toward women in general and toward certain women in particular. Carlitos told how Ceboll had Packy Tate under his thumb, because Packy—like most other people in Edmunds—was beholden to Ceboll. Shinefeld concurred with Carlitos's estimation of the man, adding that he was working on a way to help pry Edmunds loose from his grasp. "I think maybe I can get him under federal racketeering and conspiracy charges, now that we have evidence that he was pressuring a public official. I wonder how much Packy's into him for?"

"Eight thousand," said Carlitos.

"Now, how do you know that?" Shinefeld was impressed.

"He borrowed it to buy his house. My brother handled his mortgage application at Villaseca National Bank."

"It was approved?"

"Sure. The bankers like Ceboll's money as much as anybody else's."

"You're getting off the subject," objected Dewey. "Do you think he's capable of murder, Carlitos?"

Carlitos thought for a moment. "Yes and no, Mrs. James. He could kill a person, I think. But I do not think that he would commit the type of murder that we are all thinking of. Larry Ceboll is not the man to conceal his traces, or to sneak in at night to do such a thing. He would do it right out in public. And it might seem almost by accident that he had done it, if you know what I mean."

"He wouldn't plan it?"

"No, he would not plan. He would simply break the person's neck. Before witnesses, if there were witnesses. He would never care about the killing—he thinks he is right in everything he does." Carlitos shook his head. "And, I am sorry to tell you that he probably wouldn't be arrested, either. Everybody's too afraid of him."

Dewey had a good feeling for Ceboll now. Carlitos directed her to his office, and—completely ignoring the loud protests of George Farnham and Steven Shinefeld— she had Carlitos deposit her outside the door of the *Trumpeter*.

George said glumly that he and Carlitos would meet her at the donut shop in one hour.

Dewey nodded, and marched into the noxious little office.

As Dewey entered, Ceboll was hanging up the phone. He gave Dewey a look of annoyance. "Yeah?"

"Mr. Ceboll, how do you do. My name is Dewey James."

The man didn't look surprised to see her at all. Undoubtedly that had been Packy Tate on the phone, calling to tell Ceboll what had happened.

"Yeah? What do you want for that, a medal? Or a chest to pin it on?" He guffawed, then wheezed, and then spat. "Look, what do you want, lady? I'm busy, and I don't need any articles about the prize daffodil in your garden."

Dewey took a seat on a greasy vinyl chair in front of Ceboll's desk and averted her eyes from the largely porno-graphic decor of the office. She looked straight at Ceboll, looked him straight in the eye. Dewey's look could be formidable when she chose. "Since you went to such great lengths to get me here, suppose you tell me what you want with me?"

Ceboll looked away from her, pretending to search for something in the pile of papers on his desk. "Believe me, lady, there ain't nothing you could offer me that I'd want."

"Perhaps not," Dewey agreed mildly. "On the other hand, if Sheriff Tate is obliged to face charges of false arrest, I have no doubt that you might be implicated in the scenario."

Nyna-Joan Rebacker had been right on the mark with her imitation of this broad, Ceboll reflected. " 'Implicated in the scenario'?" he mimicked. "I ought to charge you a fee for using such fancy words. We're just plain folk here in Edmunds."

"Mr. Ceboll. I would appreciate it greatly if you would tell me why you went to such lengths to have Sheriff Tate take me in."

"Aw, lady, shut up and go away."

"I will not." Dewey meant it, and her determination was evident. She sat back in the chair, folded her hands in her lap, and prepared to wait.

Larry Ceboll was completely unaccustomed to defiance. He looked at Dewey curiously for a long moment, then his fat face broke into a smile. "You're all right, lady."

"Thank you," said Dewey, a little grimly. "Now, talk."

"What the hell? I guess I will!" Ceboll let out a long

laugh. When he was finished, he lit a half-smoked cigar, leaned back in his chair, and talked.

"Here's how it was," he said, gesturing with his stump of a cigar. "I figured I could find out something about why that girl died. I think she was murdered by Gerald Clearwater, who's always been a sneaky little rat, all his life. He thinks he's so much better than I am, sitting up there with his fancy friends, but he's flat broke and ready to go belly-up. So I figured he's finally cracked, and at last I'm gonna get my hands on that place."

Aha, thought Dewey. This is where the standing offer to buy comes from. No wonder Gerald and Sonia were prepared to fight to the bitter end. It would be truly dreadful to have beautiful Los Lobos fall into the hands of this disgusting creature.

She smiled blandly. "You'd like to purchase Los Lobos?"

"No. I'd like to get it for free." He laughed crudely. "But hell, if I gotta buy it, I might as well get it as cheap as possible. Problem is, people like Gerald Clearwater think they're above the law. He figures he can murder this girl and get away with it, just because he's got fancy friends. Hell, they're not his friends. He charges them a fee—they're just business. They don't give a damn about him."

Dewey reflected that this could perhaps have been true, to some degree. How hard it must be to open your house to people every day, and treat them like good friends—almost like family, really—and know that after they paid the bill they might never give you another thought.

Except that people always came back to Los Lobos—and they didn't come back just for Sidney Bachelor's food, or to ride the sweet, stubby little horses. They came back because they found Gerald and Sonia good company, and because they found Los Lobos fascinating or soothing or somehow deeply pleasing. They came back because they were more than just paying customers—they *were* friends.

Larry Ceboll, of course, could not be expected to understand such a thing.

Dewey had a sudden inspiration. She pointed a stern finger at him, just as though he were some reprobate, returning an overdue book to her beloved library. "That whole thing was your idea, wasn't it?"

Ceboll drew the cigar from his mouth and looked at it. "What whole thing?"

Dewey could see from his manner that he knew exactly what she was talking about.

"The foolishness about the ghost. That was all your doing, wasn't it?"

Ceboll laughed. "Lady, now, how did you figure that one out?"

Because you're the only person childish enough to pull such a stupid stunt, Dewey thought. "Well, if you look at it, it's obvious. The purpose of the campaign was bad publicity—the kind that could mean the end of the road for Los Lobos. The publicity takes place right here"—she tapped a copy of the *Trumpeter*—"but you need to have something to report. You can't make it up, because then Sonia and Gerald can just ignore it. So you have to have facts. But you needed to create the facts, first, in order to report them. Otherwise they could sue you for libel. Am I right?"

"You'll never prove it by me." Ceboll grinned, showing yellow teeth.

"No, I don't expect so." Dewey wasn't worried. The business with the ghost was over with, and with clever management the damage could be contained.

But the damage done by the murder of Harriet Bray was another thing altogether. She said as much.

"Why did you think I could help you?" she asked.

"I figured you would know. I heard you were kind of a detective, in your hometown."

"Now, where on earth did you hear that?" Dewey was genuinely surprised.

"Nyna-Joan told me."

That clicked, thought Dewey. "The receptionist at Dr. Little's office?"

"That's the one. She's quite a gal, Nyna-Joan Rebacker. She told me all about how Matt Little checked up on you, with the cops, and they said"—he looked at Dewey shrewdly—"they said as how you were more or less of a pain, but that you sometimes helped out, one way or another."

Dewey made a mental note to have a word with Fielding Booker on her return to Hamilton. He would have to account personally for that remark. "And you thought if you put me in jail, I would help you spread lies about my hosts up at Los Lobos."

"Not lies." Ceboll shook his head. "Hell, everybody in town knows Gerald must've killed that girl. Probably the one before her, too."

"What makes you say that?"

"Because he's been so damn stubborn about letting Packy anywhere near the place. And Matt Little. And now he's got his fancy friend Nick Hafter to protect him. The way I got it figured, he was having an affair with her, and she was gonna tell the wife, and everybody knows it's the wife that keeps that place together. So he had to kill her."

Dewey reflected that Sonia and Gerald had played a very bad hand over the death of Monica Toro. Well, there was nothing Dewey could do about that now. There was no reason on earth to believe Gerald guilty of such things—at least, so it appeared to Dewey. But the rest of the world was not bound to regard him in the same way. There were plenty of people in the world willing to be very suspicious— especially when a man Gerald's age had any kind of connection with a pert young woman like Monica Toro.

She had been up to something. Dewey was convinced of it. Harriet had felt it, and Harriet had not exactly been capable of subtle reasoning. Harriet was the kind of person who only tumbled to the truth when it hit her in the face like a cream pie.

Monica had been up to something that was going to leave her set for life—so she had confided to Harriet. To Dewey's way of thinking, that meant that Monica was going to be quite rich. There weren't many ways for a young woman like Monica Toro to become rich overnight. Either she was going to marry a million, or inherit a million, or steal a million. All things being equal, Dewey's money was on the third possibility.

She sat in thought for a moment. Larry Ceboll was clearly a loose cannon. It would be much, much smarter to harness him than to harass him.

"Mr. Ceboll, you're a newspaperman."

"Damn right." He held up a copy of the *Trumpeter*. "Best damn paper in all of the Escondida Valley."

And the only one, too, reflected Dewey. "I have an idea about all of this. How would you like to scoop the world?"

"Lady, you talk my language."

"I thought so. Now listen."

It took Dewey the better part of fifteen minutes to explain her idea to Larry Ceboll. She would have to recruit Packy Tate as well; Ceboll had promised to get him lined up to help. Ceboll saw this as his big chance. The *Foothill Trumpeter* would be bigger than the *Times*, more respected than the *Bee*, more profitable than *USA Today*. Larry Ceboll would be the next Rupert Murdoch. The next Ted Turner.

Shoot—if only he could get himself the next Jane Fonda!

*   *   *

In Mike's Donut-O-Rama, where George and Carlitos were waiting, the air was oppressive. George was partial to good donuts, but even the fresh-baked delicacies coming from Mike's couldn't alter his mood. Unless he was very much mistaken, Dewey had snubbed him. He had blazed into town to rescue her from jail, and she had barely said a word to him. She had spoken only to Carlitos and Shinefeld. She hadn't even smiled at him, and she had refused his help in dealing with Larry Ceboll. Even though he had rescued her from jail!

He felt vaguely, dimly, that if Dewey were annoyed with him he was somehow to blame, but that sensation only made him more irritated. Dewey couldn't snub him. She wasn't that kind. He must be imagining things.

22

WHEN DEWEY AND George and Carlitos arrived back at Los Lobos, no one seemed to have noticed that they had been gone. No one, that is, except for Eloise, who happened to be lounging on the front porch, and happened to see them arrive. She gave them a vague little wave, and smiled at George.

"Hail the conquering hero," she said, as they made their way up the steps. Her voice was like honey. "I understand there was some kind of trouble with the law." She giggled softly and looked curiously at Dewey, as though surprised such a thing could happen. Her attitude seemed to indicate that such things didn't happen to busy, important people.

"Hello, Eloise." George's tone was brisk and energetic.

"Well? Aren't you going to tell me all about it?"

"Later." George indicated his tennis clothes. "I'm going to go and change. See you all at lunch."

Sonia and Gerald bustled out to greet Dewey, with hugs and exclamations. "Dewey, we were terribly, terribly worried about you," said Sonia, embracing her old friend. "Thank heaven for George, that's all I can say."

"And thank heaven for Carlitos and Steven Shinefeld," amended Dewey.

"We're dreadfully sorry about all of this," put in Gerald.

"You needn't be." Dewey reassured them again that she

181

was fine and excused herself. She wanted to freshen up before lunch. Afterwards, she might not have a chance.

Once she had changed, Dewey went to the stables to look for Carlitos. She was banking on him to help. There was information that she required, and she was fairly certain that Sonia and Gerald couldn't supply it—they were too far gone with anxiety, at this point, to be thinking quite clearly about anything. Besides, they probably didn't know the answers.

Dewey herself wasn't really certain what to look for. But she knew that the answer lay in finding the cause of Monica Toro's strange exultation. And of all the people at Los Lobos, Carlitos struck her as both the most reliable and the most observant.

She found Carlitos quickly. He was grooming a little bay gelding called Fosforito, who gave Dewey a welcoming nudge with his soft nose. She thought again about Starbuck, her own sweet horse, and suddenly she longed to be home in Hamilton. She would feel much better as soon as she could get home to Starbuck and her faithful black Labrador, Isaiah.

"Mrs. James." Carlitos smiled at her. "You are quite brave, I think."

"Oh, poor Carlitos. It was actually sort of a diverting morning. But I am glad to be free, and I wanted to thank you for rescuing me."

"It was my pleasure. I would do it many times over, for such a beautiful señora." Carlitos's black eyes twinkled, and Dewey felt a pleased blush on her cheeks. It had been a long time since any man had told her she was beautiful, and she did not doubt, for a moment, that Carlitos meant what he said. He wasn't a man to throw out idle compliments.

"Carlitos, you mentioned to me the other day that you were surprised at something."

"Did I?"

"Yes. I need you to confirm it for me." Dewey talked to him for fifteen minutes. At the end, when she was certain that his recollection was unshakable, she departed. Larry Ceboll had promised that he and Sheriff Tate would arrive by one-thirty—lunchtime.

She was just in time to intercept them as they pulled up in the sheriff's car. She didn't want Sonia and Gerald to see them. She wanted to avoid, for the moment, foolish recriminations about what had happened this morning. Dewey had bigger fish to fry.

"Hiya, lady," said Ceboll, as he climbed out of the car with a can of beer in his hand. He took a long pull, dumped the rest on the ground, and crushed the can. Then he belched and hitched up his trousers. "I brought you the law."

Packy Tate was apparently still suffering from the unnerving and rather humiliating experience of the morning. After Dewey's departure, Judge Hafter had summoned him to court and demanded that he explain his behavior. The good judge had insisted that Packy offer a written, public apology, to be printed in the *Trumpeter* at Ceboll's expense, for the inhospitable and egregious way he had treated a visitor to the Escondida Valley. Now, as Packy faced Dewey, he hung his head.

"Sheriff Tate," said Dewey, in a lively tone of voice, "I suggest we let bygones be bygones." She stuck out her hand. "Now will you shake hands with me?"

"That's mighty kind of you, Mrs. James," said Packy, the relief evident on his face. "I'm feeling kind of stupid about everything."

"It's quite all right. I'm willing to believe that you took me in with the best of intentions."

"Well, I sure hoped I'd get some information out of you," replied Packy.

"In the future, Sheriff, I suggest you just ask. It's much the simplest way to get an answer. Now—did you bring that search warrant?"

"Yes, ma'am. This time it was signed by Judge Hafter. All nice and legal. He sends his regards, by the way."

"Good," replied Dewey, distracted. "I doubt we shall meet with resistance, but it is just as well to be prepared. Follow me."

She led them up the steps and into the small library, where she had sat that morning perusing Great-uncle Horacio's diary. She took the old volume down from the shelf and opened it to a page with pen-and-ink renderings of the south wing, where the staff had their rooms. She indicated the carefully camouflaged hiding places in the drawing and explained briefly about Great-uncle Horacio's career. "I don't know what you will find," she said, "but I have no doubt you will find something. The room you want to search is the third from the end. It has been locked since Wednesday."

"Uh-oh. We gotta break in?" asked Tate.

"No, indeed." Dewey reached in her pocket and withdrew a large iron key. "Here you go. I shall meet you back here in fifteen minutes."

Charles Halifax stood in the areaway that led to the old kitchen, watching the proceedings with interest. He was eating a carrot—ever since Harriet's death, he had been on a strict diet. His casual pose was contradicted by the look of tense concern in his eyes.

Sidney Bachelor, wiping floury hands on his apron, joined him. "What are those two clowns up to now?" asked Sidney. The story of Dewey's arrest had just finished making the rounds. "They're going into your room, Charles."

Charles Halifax shook his head. "Not my room, Sidney," he said, as the sheriff and Ceboll made their way along the portico. They paused outside the second door. "That's your room."

Sidney frowned. Packy Tate stood back from the door and counted, first from one direction—one, two, three—and then from the other: one, two. Dewey had told him the third room—but from which end? He shrugged his shoulders and withdrew the key from his pocket. He inserted it, and turned. Nothing.

"Not my room," said Sidney, as the sheriff moved on. One more door down. "That's the girls' room."

"What the heck does he want there?" Charles had finished his carrot. He folded his arms and watched as Sheriff Packy Tate tried the key. It worked; he opened the door and entered.

Ceboll had his reporter's notebook out. This scoop, if scoop it was, would have a real byline. Not "Special to the *Trumpeter*," but "By Lawrence Ceboll." Something he'd be proud to stick his monicker on.

"What the heck are those clowns up to?" Charles asked again.

"I know how you feel about him. Moreover, I know how he feels about you. Relax, Gerald."

Dewey was closeted in the red parlor with the Clearwaters. Gerald, looking more than ever like he'd been tumble dried, was pacing back and forth, dodging the furniture that cluttered the room. Sonia, looking cool and composed, was seated in the corner of the sofa. She had one elegant leg crossed over the other, and her hands were clasped about her knee. Dewey admired her sangfroid.

"Dewey, I think you've finally gone around the bend," Gerald said hotly. "I thought you were here to help us. To keep us out of that filthy rag he calls a newspaper, and to help us solve our problems."

"Gerald, there is more at stake here than a news article. Believe me, this would have to come out sooner or later; it's far, far better to make use of Ceboll than to let his resentment of you take the upper hand."

"Dewey is right, Gerald. As usual." Sonia gave a half smile. "I only wish she'd tell us what they're looking for."

"I don't know myself, exactly. What I've told Sheriff Tate is that we want anything, anything at all, that may have a bearing on the people here at Los Lobos. Because someone here killed Harriet Bray—and Monica Toro before her."

"That's ridiculous." Gerald was submissive.

"Is it?" Dewey's voice was calm. "I hardly think so, Gerald. Harriet Bray died because she knew something, I'm willing to wager. Just think about it. She had no sophistication, no subtleness, that girl. All she had was an earnestness that wore on everyone's nerves, and a tendency to talk nonstop about whatever came into her head."

"I'll grant you that," said Gerald. "That's no reason to be selected by a murderer."

"Well, of course it is, Gerald, if you happen to say something that could expose the murderer's previous crime."

"Wait a minute, Dewey," demanded Sonia. "You're saying that one person murdered both of those young women?"

"I am."

"Then it has to be someone who works for us. Someone in our employ." Sonia's face fell.

"A member of your staff, you mean?"

"Well, yes. Unless it's Larry Ceboll himself, and you've set him some elaborate trap."

"Let's give up the speculation, Sonia, until they've finished with their search. All right?"

"Very well." Sonia looked at her watch. "It's lunchtime. I suggest we eat."

23

AT FIVE O'CLOCK that afternoon, Sheriff Tate concluded his meeting with Dewey. Nicholas Hafter had arrived, ready to sign an arrest warrant; earlier in the day, he had also signed an exhumation order for the body of Monica Toro. As Hafter was arriving at Los Lobos, Matthew Little was examining the young woman's body. Now that he was looking for it, the broken hyoid bone was obvious. As she struggled for life in the Los Lobos swimming pool, Monica Toro had evidently been strangled. Hafter used the Hacienda's phone to call in to the medical examiner's office. The confirmation of that fact put to rest any doubts that might have lingered.

"Looks like you were right on the money, Mrs. James," said Hafter, as he hung up the phone. They had taken over Gerald's office for their conference. "Definite evidence of foul play." He shook his head. "You think we'll find this person here?"

"I'm sure of it." Dewey gestured to a pile of things on the corner of the desk. There were ten or twelve issues of *Faces* magazine, and four letters addressed to Monica Toro, care of the Hacienda Los Lobos. There was a Xerox copy of an ancient contract, as well. These documents, which Packy Tate had found in the room shared by Harriet and Monica, told a story of blackmail and extortion. They were powerful stuff—and they had been carefully secreted in one of Great-uncle Horacio's hiding places. The old bandit had had

189

a knack for concealment. The documents also spelled out a motive for murder.

"I believe the others are all waiting for us in the dining room," said Dewey. "Shall we?"

"After you," said Nicholas Hafter. They departed, with Packy Tate tagging along behind. This was going to be the biggest moment of his career.

The Los Lobos guests were all assembling around the enormous dining room table, under the watchful eye of Great-uncle Horacio. The Miltons were on the one hand sulky, because they were being obliged to join in a group activity; on the other hand, they were pleased because tomorrow was Saturday, and they could leave. Serena and Lorenzo were seated together at one corner of the table; they were babbling away to each other about a wolf spider that they had encountered on their hike this afternoon. Eloise Morningside had taken up a position in the middle of the table; she was evidently waiting for George. As he entered the room, she waved a stemmed glass in his direction.

"Margaritas," she said. "Don't you just love these exotic customs?" She patted the seat of the chair next to hers. "Come and sit down. I'm all nerves."

George obliged, but it was clear to see he didn't share Eloise's high spirits.

"Where's your librarian friend?" asked Eloise. "She gone for a tour of the Edmunds Fire Department?"

"Oh, I have a feeling she'll be along," answered George. "She usually manages to show up when she's wanted."

"How often is that?" Eloise asked musically, but her comment was lost in the noise of the crowd.

The entire staff was here as well. Mark Harris leaned up against one wall. He was, as usual, dressed in impeccable tennis whites. It was impossible to imagine that he ever wore anything else. The chambermaids aligned themselves neatly, as was their custom. They directed their gaze toward their shoes. Sidney and Beverly, both looking harried, waited impatiently by the door to the kitchen. There was a soufflé halfway finished in the kitchen; a delay would mean disaster. Their agitation was contagious—before many seconds had passed, everyone in the room seemed fidgety.

Sonia and Gerald arrived in company with Charles Halifax. He scowled at everyone and stood, aloof, in the doorway to the outside portico. He didn't plan to stay long. Two of the grooms came with him; Carlitos was nowhere to be found, he explained hastily to Gerald. Gerald waved it away, as if it didn't matter.

When everyone was more or less settled, Gerald took the floor.

"As you know, Los Lobos has been the witness to terrible tragedy lately. We have lost not one, but two, very valuable members of our staff. There is reason to believe, now, that these losses were not the result of accidents, as earlier thought, but deliberate murders."

There was a general outburst of dismay. The three chambermaids, straining to understand the English, turned heatedly to the grooms, talking in agitated voices. Mark Harris was evidently stunned. Charles Halifax looked bored. Sidney still seemed to be worried about his soufflé, but Beverly was noticeably pale. Soufflés come and soufflés go, but murder is exceptional.

Lorenzo and Serena chatted to each other, confirming what everyone had just heard. Belinda Milton's voice rang out above all the rest. "Great. That's just great," she was heard to exclaim to her husband. "Whatdaya want to bet we have to stick around this dump till they find the guy?"

Gerald looked her way as he called for order. "Mrs. Milton," he said, his voice tight and controlled, "we shall see to it that you are not greatly inconvenienced. Certainly, you shall not be as inconvenienced as the two young women who were murdered."

Belinda looked defiant, but Philip seemed chastened. "Sorry," he mumbled, and glared at his wife. "We'll be happy to help if we can."

"Thank you. Now." Gerald rubbed his hands together nervously. "I believe that our guest, Mrs. James, would like to speak to us all. Dewey?"

Dewey had just arrived, with Packy Tate and Nicholas Hafter in tow, and a belching Larry Ceboll bringing up the rear. She entered the room and looked around. Then she addressed Gerald.

"Where is Carlitos?"

"Here I come, señora," called Carlitos, squeezing past Ceboll and Tate. "Sorry to be delayed."

Dewey nodded. "That's quite all right." Carlitos took a seat on one of the chairs up against the kitchen wall. He looked agitated.

Dewey addressed the gathering briefly. She described to them the way she had reasoned, originally, that Harriet Bray had been murdered. "She was, unfortunately, a woman with too much enthusiasm," said Dewey. "She was eager. I think, when she was killed, that she actually thought she was helping to clear up the death of Monica Toro. Her enthusiasm to help was unfortunately what placed her in jeopardy."

"How so, Mrs. James?" asked Mark Harris.

"She thought that she was bringing a powerful light to bear upon the unresolved aspects of Monica's death," said Dewey. "Instead, without knowing it, she had invoked the power of darkness. I believe that with the help of Sheriff Tate, Judge Hafter, and Mr. Ceboll, that we have discovered why that was so."

There was a quiet murmur; Mark Harris leaned sideways

to translate for the chambermaids, who kept their gazes down.

"Carlitos?" said Dewey.

"Yes, señora?"

"You said something to me the other day that was quite important, but neither of us realized it at the time."

"Yes, señora."

"Yes. You said something about how skillful a rider Ms. Morningside is. But you must have been mistaken—Ms. Morningside has told me that she doesn't ride."

"No, that can't be." Carlitos shook his head in contradiction. "Of course she rides. I have seen her on a horse on these very hillsides."

"Are you certain, Carlitos? She has also stated that this is her first visit to Los Lobos."

"Perhaps she has not been here to Los Lobos as a guest. But certainly she has been here. I have seen her."

"That man's an idiot," Eloise murmured to George. "Well, a sad old thing like that, what do you expect?"

George gave Eloise a strange look.

"You saw her—when?" Dewey pursued. "Do you remember?"

Carlitos nodded eagerly. "Of course. I saw her three times." He pulled a worn-looking diary from the pocket of his shirt. "The first time was when I was breaking Fosforito. It was not long ago. We were out in the south pasture." He flipped back through his calendar. "About one month ago. Here it is. March second was the first day I worked with Fosforito. We spent three full days at it—three days and he was broken." Carlitos smiled; a job well done.

"The man keeps a horse diary?" asked Eloise, stifling a mirthful giggle.

Carlitos frowned at her. "No, señora. I started with

Fosforito on the anniversary of the death of my wife. That is a date I am not likely to forget."

There was a prolonged silence in the room. Eloise looked as though she were going to laugh again, but the look in George's eye made her go pale.

"I thought as much," said Dewey. "And the last time you saw her was March fourth, then?"

"Yes, señora. March fourth, in the evening, as I was heading for the stables. It must have been six-thirty in the evening; I was late for my supper, I recall."

"Where was she going?"

"Toward the Hacienda. She was coming up over the far ridge, and she passed within fifty yards of me. She was deep in thought, and she didn't notice me."

"No, she wouldn't have noticed you, Carlitos. She had something on her mind." Dewey turned her gaze toward Sheriff Tate. "Would you be so kind," she asked him, "to describe what you found in the room that the two women shared?"

"Sure." Packy Tate rose and hitched his trousers up. "I found a stack of magazines, New York-style gossip magazines, the one she works on." He pointed a finger.

"That doesn't mean a thing," said Eloise. She rolled her eyes. These hicks. "We sell over three hundred thousand copies a month. Everyone reads *Faces*. Well—evidently not quite everyone. Everyone but Packy Tate, the eminent sheriff of Lincoln County."

"Was there anything else?" prompted Judge Hafter. Packy Tate was never a very good witness.

"Sure. Some letters, like I told you earlier. They were to Monica Toro, but there wasn't no signature."

"And?" asked Hafter.

"Well, plus a Xerox of an old contract."

"What kind of contract?"

"It was for a legal adoption. From Mr. Ceboll's father, to some people in New York."

"Their name, Packy?" Hafter was impatient.

"Oh, sure. They were called Morningside, just like her."

There was a stir in the little room. Larry Ceboll smirked. Charles Halifax looked amused. Belinda and Philip Milton were having trouble following the significance of what Sheriff Tate was telling them.

Eloise sat stock-still, her long, elegant fingers resting against the stem of the margarita glass.

"Could somebody explain, please, what all this is about?" Philip Milton asked, in an annoyed voice.

"Yes, please do, please do," seconded Lorenzo Lee.

"Perhaps Ms. Morningside can tell us?" Dewey suggested. Eloise ignored the suggestion. "No?" said Dewey. "Well, then, I will do my best. As many of you know, Mr. Ceboll here had no brothers or sisters when he was growing up. His mother had died in childbirth. But not at *his* birth—no. At the birth of her daughter. When Mrs. Ceboll died, Larry's father did something that was quite common, half a century or more ago. He arranged for some relatives to take the second child, because he could not cope with two children all by himself. The little girl went back East, to be given a better home and raised by distant cousins. Their name was Morningside, and they were generous with their assistance with the child, who never lacked for anything. She grew up well cared for and well educated; in addition, she possessed a natural streak of ambition. By the time she was thirty years old, she was one of the most celebrated and powerful women in her field."

"Wait a minute," said Belinda, finally showing some interest. "You mean Eloise here is the sister of that guy over there?" She pointed to Ceboll with incredulity; evidently the others in the room were having a hard time believing it, too.

There was a general murmur of dissent, but Larry Ceboll's harsh voice cut through the noise.

"Damn right," he said. "That conceited, stuck-up—"

"That will do, Larry," Hafter suggested firmly.

"What's the problem with that?" asked Lorenzo Lee.

"The problem with that," responded Dewey, "is that Eloise built her reputation on being a glamorous, mysterious, and altogether superior sort of person. She was ashamed of her origins, and ashamed of her brother."

"You mean she *knew*?" asked Ceboll. He actually sounded hurt.

"Oh, she knew," replied Dewey. "Didn't you, Eloise?"

"My dear Mrs. James, this is the most fanciful concoction I have ever enjoyed in my life. Perhaps you should become one of my fiction contributors."

"Eloise knew," Dewey went on, "but she didn't want you to find out, Larry. That would have seemed, to her, like the end of the world. You would have announced the fact in the *Trumpeter*—"

"And why the hell not? Aren't I good enough for her?"

"Evidently not," said Dewey. "But then, conceit is a trait that most murderers share. Am I right, Eloise?"

24

WHEN SHE REALIZED that the game was up, Eloise Morning-side did something rather amazing. First she shrugged. Then she planted a kiss on George Farnham's cheek. "It's been fun," she told him, rising from her chair. She squeezed through the astonished crowd and marched over to Packy Tate. "Go ahead and arrest me," she said.

And he did.

Later that evening, a smaller group was gathered in the red parlor: the Lees, the Miltons, George, and the Clearwaters. They wanted to hear the rest of Dewey's story.

Dewey was pleased to oblige. "It was Carlitos, really, who solved the case for me."

"How so?" asked George. He was feeling a little blue, perhaps the result of having been kissed by a murderess.

"Because he told me that he had seen Eloise riding. Only today did I remember that she had told me she doesn't ride. Not only that, but that she had never been to Los Lobos before."

"So when did Carlitos see her?"

"When she snuck up here on horseback to meet with Monica Toro. Monica, when she was working as Larry's assistant, had seen the old adoption papers. There had been nothing secret about them, but Larry, being Larry, didn't understand the significance of the information. Monica, however, was a subscriber to *Faces* and an ardent lover of the jet-setting crowd that came through Los Lobos. She kept back issues, and circled the pictures of the celebrities that she had known through her job here. And one day, she must have realized that the fabulous, famous, glamorous woman behind *Faces* was the sister of Larry Ceboll, publisher of the *Foothill Trumpeter*."

"But what's wrong with that?" asked Belinda Milton. "I mean, he's not Prince Charming, but who cares?"

"Eloise cared," replied Dewey. "Eloise had probably known all her life where she came from and what her origins were. But she was a snob and a social climber, and the worst-case scenario, from her point of view, would be if her origins ever became common knowledge. The worst thing she could imagine was that Larry Ceboll should ever discover the truth. She knew what kind of a person he was, crude and ambitious, just like herself—they really have a great deal in common. Her reputation would have been shot, and her magazine would have been a laughingstock. You can't sell snobbery if you're not a snob yourself."

"But Monica wanted to make it public?" asked Sonia. "You mean she threatened to do so?"

"We'll probably never know whether she threatened to tell the world, or just to tell Larry Ceboll. Either way, it would have been the end of a fabulously glamorous career for Eloise. And, more importantly, it would have been the end of her own image of herself in that vein. She couldn't bear to confront herself as an ordinary mortal. Because she was Eloise, and she was fabulous."

"Really, I think people like that are so shortsighted," interjected Serena. "Don't they know that all life-forms are related?"

"How true, my dear," Lorenzo said encouragingly. "How true. From the lowest to the highest, we are all part of Nature."

"I would say she's probably about the lowest," put in Belinda Milton. "The lowest of the low."

"Wait a minute," said Philip. "Okay, I've got you so far. She came here kind of on her own, and rode a horse up here, and met with Monica. Right?"

"Right," said Dewey. "And, I imagine that Monica asked for a great deal of money. Probably this wasn't the first time she had done so, either. Of course all of that can be checked, because Monica seems to have been an organized little blackmailer. She kept careful records."

"Whew!" exclaimed Lorenzo. "People certainly can be odd creatures when they choose."

"They certainly can," agreed Serena.

"Anyway, what happened to the other girl? Harriet. What happened to her?"

"She, I imagine, was just the victim of her own enthusiasm. Do you remember our nature walk?"

"Sure," said Philip.

"Well, I recall that Harriet and Eloise had *quite* a lengthy conversation during our walk."

"So they did," agreed Serena. "Remember, Lorenzo, on the day we were looking for ant lion traps?"

"Yes, my dear, I recall it perfectly," Lorenzo said warmly. "We found some rather nice ones that day."

"Okay," insisted Philip, waving away the discussion of Nature. "So then what? What other things, Mrs. James, made you realize it was her?"

Dewey blushed slightly. "On the day that Harriet died," she said, "I collided with Eloise. She had been trying to search Harriet's room, I think, but had confused the south and west wings."

"Oh," said Sonia. There was a curious edge to her voice. She looked at George.

"What do you mean, saying 'Oh' like that?" insisted George.

"Dewey—you tell him."

"Certainly. I caught her coming out of your room, George." She looked him straight in the eye.

"My room!" George was flabbergasted. "Where was I?"

"Well, we don't know the answer to that one, do we, George?" remarked Gerald. "Since you're the only person who's been impertinent enough to ask."

"How embarrassing," commented Serena, with typical finesse. "To think that George probably thought she was *interested* in him. A glamorous, attractive woman like that."

"Er, yes," agreed George. "That would have been embarrassing—but fortunately, Serena, I don't flatter myself that she was interested. And I don't think she's all that glamorous, either. Just for the record." He looked straight at Dewey. "I didn't find her glamorous, nor attractive, nor anything at all. She simply struck me as being a bit lonely."

Belinda snorted in derision, and Philip rolled his eyes at her.

"Wait a moment," insisted Serena. "This Eloise, she sneaked into Harriet's room, when she believed Harriet would be at lunch with the rest of the staff?"

"That's right," agreed Dewey. "But Harriet was quarreling with Charles that day—like every day—and she decided to eat her lunch in her room."

"Why did Eloise want to get into the room?" asked Lorenzo.

"To recover the correspondence with Monica. She knew it was somewhere. She also knew it might be incriminating."

"What I don't see," said Gerald, "is why she came out here in the first place. Or, should I say, in the second place.

She had killed Monica Toro and gotten away with it. Why turn up?"

"The need to visit the scene of the crime," suggested Serena. "Murderers can't help themselves. They have to. It's a compulsion."

"Perhaps that," agreed Sonia. "Or perhaps she just came to clear away any evidence."

"That would be my guess," said Dewey. "She's quite a capable woman, and she nearly pulled it off."

"If it hadn't been for you, Dewey," said George, "she would have."

"Oh—no," Dewey said modestly. "The one we ought to thank is Carlitos. He's the one who saved the day."

"Hey, wait," Belinda said heavily. "I don't get it. If Carlitos really saw her three times, how come she didn't notice him even once?"

"Because she never sees people like Carlitos," said Dewey. "To her, he was just a figure in the landscape, no more noteworthy than a cactus or an acacia tree. Just a humble local type with a horse, she must have thought—if she even bothered to take him in. People like that don't count with the Eloise Morningsides of this world."

"They should learn the lessons of Nature," Lorenzo said philosophically.

"That's exactly right, my dear," agreed Serena.

Two months after the scandal hit Los Lobos, Sonia and Gerald Clearwater were riding high. The fact of the murders, once the killer had been unmasked, made Los Lobos even more attractive to those people who could afford it. Many of them were the very people Eloise had delighted in trampling upon in the pages of *Faces*, and so it was with a particularly delicious sense of satisfaction that they visited the scene of her downfall. Room rates had skyrocketed in response to the heavy demand, and still people had to be turned away. Sidney Bachelor got no rest, and Beverly successfully launched the newsletter. The first issue included George Farnham's recipe for salad dressing.

Down in Edmunds, things continued pretty much the same. Larry Ceboll's *Trumpeter* was doing very well— "Doing excellent," as Larry himself had said, although he hadn't found the next Jane Fonda and was sticking with his wife for now. He had put his plans to steal Los Lobos on the back burner for now. He'd get it one day, he warned Gerald and Sonia. But they were "doing excellent" themselves and weren't nearly so worried these days.

On the day after Eloise's arrest, Ceboll had invited Packy Tate by for the official burning of the promissory note. Packy, naturally, had believed Ceboll when he'd said he had destroyed it the first time—so he was a little bit mad with Mr. Ceboll for fooling him like that. But on the other hand he was really happy because he got to set the durned thing on fire himself, which was what he wanted. Then he treated Larry to some beers out at Molly's Foothill Paradise.

Steven Shinefeld continued to occupy his storefront office on Santa Maria. With the destruction of Packy Tate's promissory note, Larry Ceboll had needed another life to toy with. He delighted in torturing Shinefeld with the threat of eviction, and Shinefeld delighted in pretending to be frightened by it. Meantime, he had quietly bought forty acres outside of Villaseca, and he was developing plans for low-income housing and a public-services office block. Pizza Hut was interested in coming in to the area. Steven Shinefeld, it turned out, was more or less of a millionaire. Ceboll would be furious when he figured it out.

Back in Hamilton, Dewey and George had resumed their contented lives. On their return, it seemed to Dewey that the little town had never looked so beautiful, with all the spring flowers in bloom. She gave a great deal of thought to all that had passed, and she admitted to herself that she now knew why she had felt insecure out at Los Lobos. This was an important lesson for her, but she hasn't yet decided how to deal with her new self-knowledge. Meantime, she and George enjoy dining together as often as ever before, and he has offered to teach her to play tennis, which has made her very happy.

At the little library that is Dewey James's pride and joy, a new volume has been given pride of place in the Rare Book Room. This is Great-uncle Horacio's diary, which Sonia and Gerald gave her as a present. Dewey likes to take it out and look through it from time to time; she hopes one day she'll return to the Escondida Valley for another ride through the brown-and-green landscape on a feisty little horse called Mal Genio.